FIERY NIGHTS
TEMPTED

BELLA AND THE BEAST MASTER

SARAH WESTILL

FIERY NIGHTS TEMPTED

Bella and the Beast Master – Book Four

ISBN 978-1-955293-23-5

Cover Design by For the Muse Designs

OTHER TITLES BY SARAH WESTILL

GEN-HEIRS: The Guardians of Sziveria

(in reading order)

Levkaseon – A Prequel

Wintersfall

Raiventon

Kynhaven

Asherwick

Ericksen - A Wintervail Special

Survaine

Wolvenguard

Voklane (Spring 2024)

Bella and the Beast Master

Gen-Heirs world series

Frozen Flowers Fallen

Perfect Melody Silenced

Dreams Never Seen

Fiery Nights Tempted

For world maps be sure to visit www. sarahwestill.com

To get the latest updates, follow Sarah on

Instagram

@authorsarahwestill

For all the couples still finding their own fiery nights.

CONTENT WARNING:
This book contains mature content
Reader discretion is advised.

CHAPTER

ONE

HAVEN CITY, SZIVERIA
July 23rd, 802 P.C.E. (post-cataclysmic event)

BELLA RALSTON HAD LOST her husband's wolf.

Again.

Pressing her lips together, she tapped her knuckle on her chin and searched the empty greenhouse. The three-story space was in its infancy. All the trees were saplings of ornamentals that would be pruned to remain dwarves in size. Blue wisterias, purple crape myrtles, golden rain trees, blood maples, river birches, cascading willows... someday the space would be a riot of color some months and vivid green others. Shrubs and huge cement pots soon to hold flowers rounded out the winding bark path and lined the indoor creek. Decorative boulders added another outdoorsy element to the space the occupants of the building would visit regularly during the coldest winter months. Right now? The new building was still finding residents, and a landscaper was artfully planning the greenhouse.

Locating a two-hundred-pound dog in the near barren space should *not* be a challenge. Every time Bella played the game with Lunah, she lost. Markus had needed to come to find his wolf. She'd figured she had a chance down here. Apparently not. One way or another, though, she would locate the wolf on her own. Calling Markus wasn't an option. Not today.

"Lunah," Bella called out in a loud whisper, as though the few residents milling about would rush upstairs to tell her mate what she'd done. They didn't need *another* thing to fight about. Crouching down, she peered under a bench. "Lunah, where are you hiding this time?"

An internal snicker fluttered into her mind. Lunah could communicate with Bella at will, but Bella hadn't figured out how to make the connection go both ways. Perhaps she couldn't since her genetics included some long-lost Ruthenian ancestor generations ago. She had enough to bond with her husband and his wolf, but the bond was weak compared to a pure-blooded Ruthenian like her husband. The capability to bond with either of them was an amazing capability she still marveled about.

Bella growled, her competitive drive rising. "You little sneak. I'm going to find you this time." Another snicker sounded in her mind.

Bella narrowed her gaze. If Lunah could hear her voice…. "I mean it."

Hunched over, peeking around rocks and shrubs, Bella knew she must look ridiculous. Okay, if she were a wolf… A wide footbridge over the brook caught her attention. She stepped slowly onto the wooden planks and peered down the narrow slats between them. A smile spread across her face. Two golden eyes met her stare.

"Found you," she whispered.

An excited yip echoed upward. Lunah bounded out from underneath the bridge. Water sprayed and splashed around her, then she turned suddenly and leaped from the water.

"No! No, no, Lunah!" Bella squealed, holding up her hands to shield herself.

Too late. The soaking wolf landed on the bridge with a heavy thud, and a whole body shake sent water flying. Bella's pink silk shirt and navy-striped linen pants absorbed every drop, covering her with damp, random spatters. Flapping water free from her hands, Bella gave the wolf a frigid stare.

Sorry, my Bella, sorry, the wolf said along their bond.

Bella patted the spiky fur between Lunah's ears. "I wanted to play."

Found me! And you found me! Lunah pranced around, clearly delighted in the new challenge their game now presented.

"Finally," Bella said, laughing.

"... me find a Mr. Markus Ralston? He lives in this building?" a man's muffled question reached Bella.

Rising on her tiptoes, she looked over the grounds and tried to pinpoint where the voice had come from. A man's shoulders slumped, and he tried the next person walking down the path.

"Pardon, I'm trying to find a tenant here?" The woman rushed away without a word, and the man frowned and glanced around, searching for another person.

Bella debated sneaking away and allowing the man to figure out how to find her husband on his own. Lunah bumped her nose into Bella's forearm, a not-so-subtle reminder she wasn't alone. Or weak. The wolf would keep any ill-intent away. Squaring her shoulders, she headed toward the man.

A dark cashmere coat over a light silk shirt and neutral cotton pants spoke of wealth. The stranger turned an ascot cap between his hands. Dark eyes widened when he spotted her, and he rushed to meet her.

"Excuse me, please, I'm looking for—"

"My husband." Bella reached out her hand. "Bella Ralston, Markus is my husband."

Heaving out a breath, he leaned forward and braced his hands on his knees, the hat crumpling in his grasp. So styled was his cropped black hair, a strand barely moved at his rush of movement. "Oh, thank summer."

Bella waited until he'd composed himself.

She motioned in the direction of the stairs, ignoring the fist of anxiety in her gut. She wasn't ready to return to their apartment. "We're on the seventh floor."

He shoved the dark brown wool cap onto his head. "I shall follow you…" His words faded as she walked past with Lunah at her side. The massive canine tended to have that effect on people. "Both," he finished with a hushed breath.

Halfway up the stairs, he suddenly said, "I'm Terrance Weldon."

The echo of his voice startled her, and she flinched. "Nice to meet you."

"Terrance Weldon? Of Weldon Accommodations and Entertainment?" he said, rushing between them to grab the rail and lean over to see her face.

Bella shrugged. "I'm sorry, I'm not familiar with either."

"Oh." He fell back. "Perhaps Mr. Ralston will have heard of me."

Bella kept a quip to herself. Markus tolerated arrogance less than she did. Mr. Terrance Weldon of Weldon Accommodations and Entertainment would learn soon enough. On the top floor, she opened the door, and Lunah sat at her side, watching Terrance with intelligent golden eyes.

Terrance turned sideways and went through the entry as far from the wolf as possible. His shoulders bumped the frame, and he pointed. "Right, this way then?"

Bella really hoped the guy wouldn't be offering an investment pitch. The relief at having located his query said he had something important more to see Markus about than a sale. Then again... a job was a job, and needing a break was something she understood all too well.

The door opened before they were halfway down the hall. Markus's massive form took up the entire space. One hand rested on the door's edge while the other locked to the frame. He'd braided his dark hair since she'd left, the thick plait laying over his shoulder to rest in contrast against his light gray shirt. Concern and an intense protective need shivered like a caress along her nerves, displacing the unease from their earlier argument. The one that had sent her stomping like a teenager from their home, Lunah on her heels.

His gaze moved past the stranger and met hers. A banked fire. The same stubbornness from earlier shone in his golden irises, along with regret. Under his unwavering focus, she was reminded of her importance. She wrapped her arms around her waist and frowned, forced to acknowledge having left as she did must have been difficult for him. Every instinct would have demanded he follow. Yet, he hadn't. Respecting her need for space. He shifted his attention to their guest.

Bella lifted a hand. "This is Terrance Weldon. He needs to speak with you."

Terrance snapped his cap from his head.

"Terrance Weldon, of Weldon Accommodations and Entertainment."

Markus glanced at Bella again, brows raised. She gave a helpless shrug.

"Ah," Terrance said in disappointment. "You haven't heard of me, either, I see." He shoved the hat back on. "Well, no worries. Doesn't matter, I suppose. I've been told you're the man to see when one needs answers."

Markus shifted from the doorway. "Please, come in."

Terrance nodded and slipped into their apartment. Lunah followed, making Bella wonder if Markus had asked her to look after their guest. Bella met him in front of the partially closed door, giving them the illusion of privacy in the empty corridor. He took her hand, lacing their fingers together. As with every time they touched, a thrill raced through her blood straight to her center. She wanted to be closer. She wanted his skin under hers. Every inch.

He sucked in a long inhale through his nose, nostrils flaring. Pulling her closer, he stuck his face into the bend of her neck and scented her again. "I'm sorry, *krahet'sna*. This is not any easier for me."

A tremble of desire quivered deep in her belly. "I know. We can discuss it more after our guest leaves."

"Discuss?" he asked, lifting his head and meeting her gaze.

Heat flamed across her cheeks. "Yes. Discuss."

Markus pushed the door open. "Do you know what he wants?"

"I have no idea, only that he was desperate to find you."

"Interesting." He motioned inside the frame. "Shall we?"

She rose on her toes and pressed a quick kiss to his mouth. "I love you."

He grabbed her faster than she could react and hugged her. "*Dsi tse'reaga mie mirsvet.*"

The fierceness from earlier returned. The delicate shiver of awareness of an emotion not her own. She was still learning to sort them out whenever he opened their bond, which he'd been doing less and less. One of the many things they'd been fighting over. Three months into their completed mating bond, they were learning the many twists and turns of life together. Not every day was a good day.

"Tell me," she whispered.

"I just.... You are my whole world," he translated from his Ruthenian words. "I don't ever want you to feel as though you don't matter."

Is that what she'd done when she'd walked away from him? Bella rested her forehead on his chest. "I never meant to make you feel that way. I'm—" She sighed. "I'm frustrated."

He rubbed his hands up her back and kissed her head. "I know. We'll sort it out."

She took a centering breath and pulled

away. Markus closed the door gently behind them. Terrance stood studying the many sketches of an underground archeological site in Thanzia that Bella had framed and hung on the dominant wall of the room. The open floor plan for the living space was divided by thick columns for the dining room and a long bar for the kitchen. Floor-to-ceiling windows filled the space with natural light. Hallways on opposite sides branched off to lead to other rooms in the large apartment.

"These are quite extraordinary. Where did you purchase them?" Terrance asked, pointing at the sketches.

"They were a gift," Markus answered.

Terrance smoothed a hand down the seam of his jacket. "My establishment in Extilis Square, I'm sure you've seen it, Crystal Sunrise Resort and Luxury? My patrons love new and exciting visuals. I have an acquisitions expert who travels the inhabited world to procure rare and unusual items for my many properties. How much?"

Markus glanced at Bella and then back to Terrance. "How much for what?"

Bella leaned close and whispered, "I think he wants to purchase the sketches."

"Or does he wish to hire us to find him more sketches?" Markus asked.

"No, I-I'm not here to hire you for acquisitions. I have someone for that already. But these are unique, yes?" He waved over the sketches.

Bella clasped her hands and offered a patient smile. "The Thanzian Institute of History sells them. There is, in fact, an entire book worth of them. Thanzia has many beautiful and colorful items to offer. I'd recommend sending your employee there next. Our copies are not for sale."

"Thanzia? I know an importer who trades with them. Brooks Coaten? He owns Coaten Cotton and Silks?" Terrance looked between them with big eyes. When neither of them said anything, his shoulders slumped, and he shook his head. "No?"

Markus sighed and went to the couch. Sitting, he opened his palm as Lunah joined him, plopping her rear on the floor, her silver tail flaring out on the carpet behind her. "How exactly can we help you, Mr. Weldon?"

Clutching his hat, Terrance went around the large, square wooden table in the center of their living room. He sat on the opposite couch, brushing his fingers along a bright blue throw pillow. "Wonderful craftsmanship. Lavish Interiors?"

"Lavish what?" Markus asked, exasperated.

Bella sat next to her husband and patted his thigh. "No, Hayden's Warehouse."

Terrance recoiled. "But this apartment is extraordinary. Why would you go to a bargain place like Hayden's?"

"Why would I pay ridiculous prices at Lavish?" Bella quipped.

"Did you come here to try to purchase

memories and insult my home, or do you have an actual purpose?" Markus asked, his eyes flashing.

Terrance visibly swallowed and slowly eased his hand from the pillow. "I have a situation. Three of my establishments have burned in two months. Two hotels and a curtain show house. I can't afford for another to be damaged or destroyed. I need to know who's targeting my businesses." He reached into his jacket and pulled out a folded slip of paper. "I have a list of suspects, but the authorities wouldn't take me seriously. They said fires happen in Haven City all the time, and they're rarely nefarious."

Markus leaned across the table and accepted the list. "You think they were set on purpose?"

CHAPTER

TWO

B ELLA CHEWED ON HER BOTTOM LIP, WAITING FOR Terrance's reply. The man sat, fingertips steepled together and pressed to his mouth. He regarded the list in Markus's hand as though he were carefully choosing his words.

"I am not outright accusing anyone of foulness," Terrance said. He held up one finger. "However, I have had some, shall we say, misunderstandings of a professional nature with most of them."

Markus raised a brow.

Terrance scoffed and glanced away. "Very well, all of them. I've had some issues with all of them, all right?"

Bella stood. "I'll go get a file."

As she headed toward their shared office, Markus said, "You'll have to be very specific, or we can't help you."

"I'm aware. Please tell me you'll..." his words faded into a garbled murmur between walls.

We.

A smile touched her lips. Always *we* when Markus referred to work *he* had been sought out for because he wouldn't take a case without her. Not unless he didn't have a choice. He'd even requested she quit her job to be his assistant on investigations. Something she couldn't bring herself to regret, even if she did still find herself wholly unqualified. However, she also couldn't deny they made a great team.

She gathered the items necessary for opening an investigation. Since they'd returned home from Thanzia, they'd helped find a missing heirloom vase, stopped a bakery rivalry from going to extremes, and recovered rare irises having been dug up and pilfered by a neighbor's mischievous dog. This was looking to be their first serious case in months. A break Bella was thankful for. The Thanzian case had taken a lot out of them both. They'd needed the easy jobs to recover.

Back in the living room, Bella handed Markus the file and his notebook. They'd both take notes. In the handful of cases they'd worked together, she'd learned they found importance in different things. She settled near him on the couch with her pen and notepad. His shoulders stiffened, and she squeezed her eyes shut and made to rise again.

"No, don't," he whispered, his hand resting on her leg.

Bella glanced at him. Tight lines bracketed his eyes and mouth. "Are you sure?"

He nodded and squeezed her knee before focusing on their newest client. "Start from the beginning."

Terrance swiped a trembling hand down his mouth. "I was in the last building when it caught fire."

"Is that why you think it might be an enemy?" Markus asked as he wrote.

"Who else would burn down my building with me inside?" he asked, hands open.

"Maybe it was a coincidence," Bella offered. "Do you live in that building?"

Terrance shook his head. "No, my house is not far from here."

"Who, besides your employees, would have known you'd be visiting the property that day?" Markus asked.

"I don't tell anyone when I'll be visiting. I like to see how my employees work without knowing the boss is coming," he said.

"So maybe a disgruntled employee," Markus said. "I'll need a list of all your business names and locations, everyone who works in your buildings, and those you've released from duty in the last year."

"A-all right, I can do that for you, though it may take a few days."

"A few days is fine," Markus assured. He pushed the list closer to Terrance. "Tell me about the ones you suspect the most."

Terrance leaned forward, bracing his elbows on his thighs. He went down the list, airing grievances. Bella pressed her lips together. Apparently, they were all suspects, in his opinion. No one was spared from what amounted to gossip. Only two jumped out for her. Gerall Burnsea and Roane Hulbert. Gerall had outbid him on a hotel property. Roane built a rival business across the street.

Bella tapped her pen on the pad. "Did your business across from Mr. Hulburt's burn?"

Terrance cleared his throat and shifted on the couch. "Uh, no. No, Elegance and Lace has not had an incident. Yet."

"And has anything happened concerning the owner that makes you suspect him specifically?" Bella asked.

Anger darkened Terrance's face, and he lifted his chin. "Roane's Enjoyment Entertainment has attempted to sabotage my business on multiple occasions. He's hired men to hold up signs that say skip tasteless elegance and too much lace, encounter real entertainment here. He's left flyers in my privacy booths that insinuated my customers had no stamina since they preferred my five minutes time allotments to his seven. Men and women now dance in his windows with fabric hanging from the ceiling to allow them to show glimpses of their bodies when people walk by. It's obscene and not to the caliber of our fine industry."

Bella had to bite the inside of her cheek, wondering what constituted obscene in the adult entertainment industry. Wasn't indecent the point? Then again, perhaps there were agreed upon standards, and Roane broke them to gain clientele.

"Has he made any threats?" Markus asked.

"Only that I was wasting my time opening across from him." Terrance smirked. "Obviously not, since he's trying to get his customers back."

"How long have you been there?" Markus asked.

"A year next month."

"And when did you have the altercation with Mr. Burnsea?"

"Just before last Wintervail."

"And the first fire was two months ago?"

"Correct."

Markus glanced at Bella. "Anything to add?"

She looked over her notes and shook her head. Markus rose and saw Terrance to the door. The two spoke in low tones for a few moments. Bella tensed at the faint *click* of the door closing. Alone together, they'd have no choice but to confront the tension between them. The immature part of her wanted to disappear down to the greenhouse again. Ignore the issues they were having so early in their relationship.

Something must have given her away. Her expression. Their bond. Markus leaned against the front door, blocking any hope of escape, arms crossed. Bella pressed her hands to her thighs and wiped away nervous sweat. How ridiculous. She was an adult. Yes, marriage was new to her, but using that as an excuse was unacceptable. No, the biggest problem wasn't so much the newness to love but rather the unrestrained access to her husband. Except for once a month, during her ovulation phase, which she currently found herself in. Then, she had zero-to-limited access and frustration.

"I want you," Markus growled from the other side of the living room, still bracing his back to the door. The muscles in his upper arms and chest shifted as he tensed at his declaration. "I've tethered my bond because two of us in a constant state of desire would be a nightmare."

Bella squirmed, her already primed body pulsing to instant life at his words. She swallowed against the urge to launch herself at him and remained planted on the couch. "And the other times?"

"I know at times I've been overwhelming you. I worry..." He glanced away and took a deep breath. "I worry I influence you, too."

"Influence me how?"

"If I'm angry, it adds to your anger. If I'm frustrated, you'll catch the rebound, like Lunah does if our bond is open. And if I'm aroused—"

Bella recoiled and slashed a hand through the air. "Stop. You think because I've experienced your need for me, you've somehow overridden my own emotions and made me some zombie wife?"

"I do not ever want to take away your will,"

he said quietly. "It's possible in my country, which is why the female initiates the bond. After? Both males and females hope they made a good choice in their mate because emotional restraints are real. With my bond being stronger than yours, I have no idea how much of me you receive."

Bella rose and crossed the distance between them. Standing before him, she met his worried stare. She pressed a fist to her chest, over her heart.

"When I feel you, I feel you all over, but in my heart? I wish I could explain how being so connected to you takes all my fears away. Even when you're mad at me, because I know, without a word spoken, what's going on with you. And when you look at me, and your love fills me?" She took a deep breath to stop the sudden sting of tears. "Markus, I have never been given more power. I wondered if I'd done something for you to stop trusting me with so much of yourself."

He uncrossed his arms and grasped her jaw in one hand and the side of her neck in the other. "Never. You are the only person I trust with all that I am."

Bella wrapped her hands around his thick forearms. "Then trust me with all that you are. If I can't handle it, I'll tell you."

Taking a deep breath, he rested his forehead on hers. "I'm leaving in a week or two. I told Terrance, and he still wants to work with us. I tried—"

Bella kissed him. They'd known a Ruthenian official would come knocking on their door. The agreement for Markus to leave the nation to marry a Sziverian was ten years of service during the non-winter months when they needed his specific investigative skills. They'd had almost three uninterrupted months. "It'll be fine. If we don't solve the situation by the time you leave, I'll keep working and apprising him until you return. I didn't quit my job for nothing."

"I'm not worried about him."

Bella smiled and caressed a hand along his bearded jaw. "I'll be okay."

He took hold of both her hands and pressed his lips to her knuckles. "I know. I'm worried about the full force of my bond influencing you."

Frustrated, Bella tried to free her hands, but he tightened his grip. "We just talked about this."

"No, we talked about you telling me if it was too much," he said.

"And I said I'd tell you—"

A wave of sexual need slammed into her like a tidal wave. She would have fallen to her knees if Markus hadn't wrapped her in his arms and hugged her to his chest.

"This is what I've been keeping from you," Markus whispered into her ear.

Held to his body as she was, every rapid beat of his heart thumped against her chest. The hard length of his erection pressed into her belly. She wanted his mouth on hers, her legs wrapped around his hips, her hands clutching his back as he surged into her. *She wanted everything.*

His lips moved to her neck, where he licked a path along her thudding pulse. "Summer sun, you smell amazing. Sugar and vanilla and berries. So much stronger when you're ready for me."

If she were any readier, she'd combust. Desire soaked her panties and made her ache. Her own, intensified by what she knew he felt. "*Markus.*"

Spinning her around, he pinned her to the door. "I'm leaving in a week, maybe a bit longer."

She grabbed his biceps and rose onto her tiptoes. "I know."

"Bella, *mie krahet'sna*, if we are together, you *will* become pregnant."

Bella clasped his face between her hands and searched his burning gaze. "Would it be so terrible?"

CHAPTER

THREE

Would Bella, round with his child, be so terrible? Absolutely not. Markus could think of nothing he wanted more. He did, however, have a very personal problem. "I know it may be selfish of me, but when you learn you're carrying my baby, I want to be here. I want to share that moment with you, not have you learn alone."

She released an uneven breath. "That's very fair. Now my turn." She held up a hand when he opened his mouth. "I'm not sleeping alone when you're in the country. I know the last two months you've felt it necessary during my ovulation phase since we hadn't talked about starting a family, but no more."

The sweet, tempting scent of her caused a shiver of lust to race through his body. The fertile time of the month for her compounded the issue, causing his body to become equally prepared for them to create a new life together.

Sexual frustration had taken on a new meaning now that he was mated.

Sleeping together would spell disaster.

He'd learned, however, Bella didn't shy away from anything having to do with intimacy between them. Forthright conversations didn't phase her. No, often, Markus was the one having the restraint issues. An unexpected personality trait he hadn't known he possessed until faced with an adventurous partner. All his previous lovers had expected and often demanded, an impersonal mating attempt. Two weeks of both parties voicing relationship expectations and the female deciding if he was worth her time. Some had, and he'd rejected their request because the woman hadn't been a good fit for *him*. Bella had taken him by complete surprise. Something he was beginning to believe she'd always be able to accomplish.

Tilting his head to kiss her neck, he slid his hands down her hips and around to her butt, grasping handfuls of her perfect shape. "I won't be able to stop myself from taking you when I'm half asleep and too desperate to realize what I'm doing. That's why I sleep in another room. Just this last time. When I return home, we'll figure out another way."

She moaned and lifted a leg to wrap around his thigh, opening her hips to cradle him exactly where he wanted to be. "Either you stay in our bed, or you'll find me wherever you are. I'm done treating my ovulation phase like some punishment for us to have to endure."

Right now, he found the comparison apt. Torture came in many forms, and a worse one than being denied the pleasure of his wife didn't come to mind. "This is important to me. I don't know how long Ruthenia is going to require of me. I could be home in two weeks or the full month they require, which would put me gone for almost two months after traveling."

Her leg slipped down, and he moved his hands to her lower back. She took his jaw between her hands, sliding her thumb along his bottom lip. "I know. We'll figure it out. We'll wear clothes to bed and promise to be in separate spaces when we shower, okay? We're adults. We can exhibit self-control."

Markus lifted a brow.

"We can!" she said, laughing. "It's three days."

"In the same bed, it will be a very long three days."

She leaned back and looked at his chest, walking her fingers down the front of his shirt. She fiddled with a button. "We can do other things."

Markus caught her hand and kissed her knuckles. "We turn all those *other things* into foreplay. Tell me one time we've been able to stop?"

A fine mist of sweat beaded along her hairline, evidence of her fight to control her physical reaction to his bond and her heightened libido. Hating the added struggles he inflicted on her through their connection, he began to pull back. She grabbed his braid and tugged.

"Don't you dare," she growled.

"Bella—"

"No. You don't get to decide for me what's too much. I'm managing, aren't I? I haven't ripped off my clothes or yours. I haven't stuck my hands down your pants."

Dropping his head back, Markus squeezed his eyes shut. How he wished she'd do all those things. Which was why sleeping in the same bed was a terrible, horrible plan. How were they going to make it three damn days, let alone nights? "You swear you'll tell me if it becomes too much?"

The hold on his braid loosened. "I promise."

They needed a distraction, and an arrogant business owner had left one sitting on their living room table. Untangling himself from his seductive wife, Markus looked at the start of the investigation, waiting for them. "Where do you want to start on this case?"

She closed her eyes and took a long, slow breath. "The paper, I think. Fires are usually written about. One of the articles may have some information Mr. Weldon was unaware of."

"Archives?" he asked, familiar now with how Sziveria managed their vast collection of non-bound printed material.

Bella nodded. "Yes, and we should research

both papers. I know *The Havener* isn't much more than gossip, but..."

"Most gossip has a thread of truth."

"Sometimes I think *The Havener* has more tenacious journalists, too. They want the stories that allure the reader, versus inform like *Haven City Chronicle.*" She laughed as she pushed off the door. "But, if I want to know what's happening with Nick, I need only look in the social pages of *Haven City Chronicle.* They're the only reliable source for guardian gossip. Their stellar reputation allows them into the most powerful of homes."

Markus followed her to the couch but didn't sit. Not trusting himself near her on a surface easy to get her vertical. "If you want to know about Nick, all we have to do is show up at Wolvenguard and ask."

She tucked a loose curl behind her ear. "I know. I was using him as an example. As an arch guardian, he wouldn't let anyone from *The Havener* into his house. But if someone from *Haven City Chronicle* knocked on his door, he might entertain a question or two, depending on the subject matter. Employees for Mr. Weldon? They'll talk to anyone who offers a few raimarks."

Markus gathered his things together. "Then let's hope something was revealed."

Certain they wouldn't need Lunah for the research, Markus silenced their bond and put her in the modest greenhouse sunroom off their bedroom. The space was mostly hers now from the waist down and where she preferred to sleep during the summer season. While cold at night, the high thirties and low forties were comfortable for the wolf compared to the nights in Ruthenia, where frost still blanketed the landscape across the country every morning in the summer. She enjoyed being able to see outside and have a window or two open for fresh air. Markus loved he could provide such for her. Their life in Sziveria may still feel unfamiliar, but they were both learning to appreciate the differences.

Lunah stretched, paws forward, tail in the air, yawning. Her sharp, white teeth flashed in the afternoon light streaming through the windows. After a full body shake, she found her sleeping pad and lay, her tail curling around her form.

"*Vestizha ksyor,*" he whispered. Her ears twitched, and she let out a short yip. He knew she'd behave herself, but giving the order never hurt.

Bella waited for him at the door. She'd donned her leather messenger bag and a crimson knit scarf loosely around her neck. He grabbed his bag off the back of a dining chair and packed the notebook and file he'd started into an outer compartment. As a last-minute thought, he grabbed his coat and shoved it inside. Opening the door, Bella raised a brow.

Motioning to the front of his pants, he said, "I can't control my reaction around you right now. We don't need that level of attention."

She bit her bottom lip. "I could—"

Markus leaned around her and closed the door, checking to ensure the lock engaged. "No point. In fifteen minutes, I'll be ready to go again. We'll deal with it, right? Like you said. Come on, we have things to discover, hopefully."

FOUR

A PLUME OF DUST BILLOWED IN THE AIR AS BELLA dropped a stack of papers. She coughed and waved the debris clear.

Markus leaned back and took in her haul. "How far back did you go?"

Bella coughed again and sat. "Six months. I had to go downstairs to long-storage to get the older publications. They only keep thirty days up here."

Markus raised a brow. "Six months? Are the curtain show houses even open in January?"

"No, and the paper only releases monthly during November, December, January, and February *if* they can safely travel. Otherwise, those months are released when it's safe to deliver. So, in January and February, the news is condensed. With all the fires and woodstoves burning, I figure those two months will give us a good baseline for how often building fires are occurring and being reported."

He tipped the seat back and regarded

her with a bit of an arrogant smirk that had her frowning. Pride trickled between their bond.

"What?" she asked when he continued to observe her across the table quietly.

"How you still think investigating isn't where you should be working confuses me."

Bella sorted through the many stacks, separating the two publications chronologically. "Knowing to look for what's normal to find what's abnormal isn't any special gift. It's common sense."

"I do not see anyone from Sziverian National Investigative Division or Haven City Enforcement Services researching papers, do you?" he asked, arms wide.

Flexing her jaw, Bella adjusted the stack of *Havener* papers before adding another two. "They don't think a crime has been committed."

Markus leaned forward, the chair legs landing with a heavy *thunk*, and braced his arms on the table. "You aren't convinced, either."

Bella snapped her head up and met his golden stare. "I didn't... I never said that."

He stretched a hand across the space and brushed her fingers. The tantalizing surge of energy that always seemed to exist between them tingled along her hand. "You didn't have to, *krahet'sna*. Your doubt was no different than my own."

Frowning, she laced their fingers together.

"What made you think he might not be being truthful?"

"When every person was a suspect. What about you?"

She squeezed his hand before releasing him and returning to her sorting. They had limited time at the archives. Once the sun set enough to restrict light, the building closed. No open flames were allowed inside. Downstairs, those searching for items in long storage were given a glowing green jar that used the same chemical reaction the First Intelligence Office utilized for their discrete night missions. Bella hated going downstairs, where the entire space was one dark void except for her little green glowing circle. Thankfully, the area was labeled well and organized, with large signs for all the categories.

"Three businesses burning down in two months being dismissed by the authorities is odd to me. I could see one, perhaps two, but three? Why would they ignore an obvious attempt at sabotage?"

Markus shrugged. "Depends. If they did indeed ask some questions and came away with a candle tipping over, a patron at the curtain show getting a little too excited and dislodging a lamp, the reasons for the fires are endless. They really could have been accidental."

"If they bothered to check, a report would have been filed. Another avenue to look into." She pushed a stack across to him. "You check

The Chronicle, and I'll look through *The Havener*."

"Why do you get the fun paper?" he grumbled.

Bella snickered. "Because I did all the hard work."

He glowered and sucked air through his teeth, the tip of his tongue making a quick appearance. Bella shivered. Using his tongue to convey an emotional state wasn't his only talent with that particular part of his anatomy.

Unbidden, a fantasy crept into her mind. No one was around, as usual. They had the area to themselves. If he were to slide under the table, tug her pants down to free one leg, spread her thighs, and use that wicked mouth of his, she'd let him. Closing her eyes, she squirmed at the sudden heat and dampness between her legs. Oh yes, and while he pleasured her, she'd do everything in her power to remain quiet.

A heavy *thunk* had her eyes popping open. Markus's head was on the table, his braid in an S configuration over the open paper. He bumped his forehead to the surface repeatedly. A flush heated her cheeks, and she shoved the erotic thoughts away.

"I'm sorry," she whispered.

"We are never going to make it through this case," he said, lifting his head enough to meet her stare.

Frustrated, she pressed her lips together to avoid saying something she'd regret. *She* didn't care if she discovered she was pregnant alone.

In fact, a tiny part of her preferred to be the only one to know because then she'd have time to prepare for the possibility of his disappointment. He'd left his home for her. The people, culture, customs, and yes, the ability to have a full-blooded heir.

Being faced with the reality of a half-blood, who-knows-what-talent may hit him differently when she opened her mouth to say the words. Selfishly, she wanted a little time to get used to the idea first. Pregnancy was welcome and desired, even if he wasn't home when she discovered his seed had created life between them. A revelation she'd made her first ovulation cycle. She really, *really*, wanted to have Markus's baby. However, she loved her husband enough to respect something so important to him.

"I'll be more careful with my thoughts," she promised.

He rose, scrubbing his hands down his face. "*Betyna,* I don't want you to worry about your thoughts. You have no idea how much I enjoy knowing you desire me. I'm just—" He dropped his hands to the table, palms up. "I'm hanging by a thread right now."

"I'm beginning to hate this time in my cycle," she muttered.

"I am sorry," he said softly. "It won't always be this way for us. We will learn with time how to best handle the intensity."

Until then, they'd both suffer and ache. Fantastic.

"I told you life with me would not be easy," he said, still low. "And now it's too late for regrets."

Bella's heart twisted painfully. She launched across the space between them, not caring about the stacks of papers sliding into a jumbled mess. She grasped his face between her palms and kissed him. A hard press of her lips. "I regret nothing."

The discomfort in her chest eased. He grasped her upper arms to hold her place, deepening the kiss she pressed to his mouth again. Without a second thought, she opened for him, needing the intimacy. The limited physical contact wouldn't be enough, not for three more days, but the sensation of his tongue gliding along hers calmed the turmoil. A sort of grounding instead of the burn of desire. Bella was learning the unexpected happened between them. Sometimes, a kiss enflamed. Sometimes it pacified.

Markus pulled a few more gentle kisses from her lips before easing back, running the pad of his thumb over her swollen bottom lip. "You will get a break from this frustration while I'm gone, at least."

Bella returned to her seat, sighing. "I'd rather be frustrated with you."

Markus plopped his elbow on the table and his chin on his hand. He smiled, his dimples making an appearance. "You say the sweetest things to me."

She laughed and tapped her toe to his shin

under the table. "You know what I mean."

"*Dak*, I know." He straightened and pulled a paper closer. "Let's see if we can find anything useful."

She'd much rather continue their teasing and frivolous banter. Too many recent, serious aspects of their relationship had stolen the playful moments. But they had a task to complete now, on limited time. Nothing new for them. Bella needed to focus and not lament things outside of their control.

With each paper, she went straight to the public information section, which listed enforcement reports and accusations for witnesses to stand for or against an accused person. The section was always printed in smaller letters. On some days, the information could take up several pages. Winter usually saw very few reports, but come March, when people could travel safely to their local enforcement division, accusations often required special printing. The Accusation Issue. This year had needed one. Lots of turmoil over the frozen season. No accusations about arson, however. Bella set the issue aside and went to the next daily. Three days after *The Havener* returned to daily printing, an article ran about a hotel catching fire. Bella drew her brows together and leaned closer to the paper.

"What are the names of Mr. Weldon's hotels?" she asked, holding her finger under the establishment's name in the article.

Papers shuffled. "The Inn at Everflow and

Haven Star Hotel."

Bella tapped her finger under the name of the hotel. Not the same. She set the paper in the chair beside her and moved on. Nine more issues made the review pile. After the last daily, she retrieved the ones that had been promising.

She picked up her pen, holding it in her hand as she related the information to Markus. "Two weeks after the last snow, *The Havener* reported on a fire at The Sizzle Show curtain show establishment. Two weeks later, to the day, they reported on a hotel fire at Park View Inn. Two weeks later, another curtain show, Velvet and Candlelight, suffered a minor fire." She flipped through the papers. "Every two weeks, it's either a curtain show or a hotel. No other fires were reported except for two residential fires, one in The Rows."

"I have that as well," he said, tapping his pen to his notebook. "Five curtain shows and five hotels, all spaced at two weeks according to the articles."

Their eyes locked across the table. Uneasiness swept through her. "The last fire, Mr. Welston's Haven Star Hotel, was set on the twelfth."

The pen continued to *tap-tap-tap* on the paper. "We have three days to find the curtain show that is next."

"Where do you want to start?"

Bella's question hung in the air between them. Markus tossed the pen down and leaned back in the chair, making the wooden legs groan. "Did your articles give any additional information about the fires?"

She laughed, tugging a paper from the bottom of a small stack near her. "Only what you'd expect from *The Havener*." She cleared her throat and leaned forward. "There was a blaze at The Sizzle Show last night. No one is certain how the inferno began, but this journalist would like to note all the ladies I spoke with were certainly hot enough to set any fire. Don't worry, none of the sultry show workers were injured. The situation, unfortunately, led to the complete destruction of the property in question. The owner would like to assure our readers he plans on rebuilding as soon as possible."

"Nothing else?" he asked.

She shook her head. "No. But Rylan Galloway, the journalist covering the ordinary in the city, *did* note an interesting pattern when Silk Drape Lounge caught fire that things are, and I quote, 'heating up in a fiery way at Haven City's curtain show houses, and not in a manner the owners anticipated when they opened.'"

"He didn't give any other speculation?" When she shook her head again, Markus stroked his beard in thought. "Odd. That publication loves conjecture."

"To be fair," she said, picking through several papers, "this journalist rarely writes his opinion on anything he reports. He does write in the required cheeky style, but that's it. They must save the speculation for the gossip section."

"Which is their entire paper."

Bella held up the *Happenings in Haven City* section of the paper. "Not the entire. What about you? Did the ever-serious *Chronicle* have anything worthwhile to report?"

"No. The articles read like enforcement reports. Date, location, and where in the building the fire had to be terminated if that information was available. For most, it wasn't. No interviews. No curiosity. At least *The Havener* seemed to make the connection between the fires."

"Where the curtain show houses are concerned, yes, but nothing about the hotels."

"There may be accidental fires at those enough to shrug them off," Markus surmised.

Bella smoothed her hands over the paper open before her. "Yes. But the two-week pattern...."

Markus nodded. "I agree. Especially with Mr. Weldon being concerned. If his hotels regularly had fire issues, he wouldn't be worried about sabotage." Rising, he organized the papers into their original issues and stacked them for the volunteers to re-categorize. No one was allowed to reshelve items at the archives except those who worked within the building. "We need a list of owners for the establishments and find out who hasn't had a property affected and who owns the same businesses."

His beautiful wife didn't move, and he paused mid-stack, raising his brows in question.

She huffed out a long sigh, her frustration zinging along their bond. "You want to research *every* hotel and *every* curtain show house in this city?"

"We have to know who's affected and who isn't."

"This is the largest city in Sziveria."

"*Dak.*"

"Everyone comes here for official business. They travel, sometimes days, from whatever port they arrive in to come *here*," she tapped the table, "to negotiate peace treaties or business deals. There are dozens of hotels in this city."

"And probably only a handful of owners. Those wealthy enough to purchase and maintain properties are few," Markus said patiently.

He knew her frustration wasn't specific to him or even the case. Rather a mashup of everything compounded together and seemingly outside of her control. She had limited experience dealing with not only his emotional state, which was unpredictable and intense during her ovulation phase but also the mechanics of an in-depth investigation. They'd done a handful of complex cases, some more than others, but nothing that required tedious research.

"You must have had to gather research for that guardian you worked for at the SNID," he said, shoving his notebook and pen into his pack.

"*That* guardian? Guardian Avner, you mean?"

Markus had another name for the arrogant coward. "Did you research for him?"

"I gathered useful evidence from C.G. when necessary, yes."

"You did all the hard work. This is the same thing, only starting at the very beginning instead of in the middle, where you often assisted."

She dropped her head in her hands, sighing again. "I'm sorry."

The sudden sting of her aggravation pulled at him. Markus couldn't stop from rounding the table, turning her chair to face him, and crouching before her. He slid his hands up her thighs, ignoring the spark of awareness. Even through clothes, touching her had a certain power over him. He gripped her hips and met her somber gaze.

"You can be upset. Isn't that what you told me in Thanzia when I apologized? We'd figure this, us, out? We aren't going to get everything right in a few months, Bella." He squeezed her hips. "We may not even get it right in a few years. I love you, and we will keep learning, *dak*?"

"Yes," she whispered.

He leaned forward enough to press a swift

kiss to her mouth before standing. Comforting warmth wrapped around his heart and flowed through his veins. The physical manifestation of her love for him.

Bella grasped his hands when we went to pull away. "I love you, too."

Smiling, he bent to give her another kiss. "I know, *krahet'sna.*" Straightening, he released her hands. "Where do we go from here?"

"Um." She chewed on her bottom lip, looking over the papers. "Probably the records department. They should have the ownerships on file."

Markus waited while she packed her notes and slipped the strap of her messenger bag over her head. They took a hired carriage to the records department, sitting opposite because he didn't trust himself beside her. Not while enclosed in the semi-private vehicle where his every touch would be hidden from outside view. Thankfully, the ride was only a few blocks. The time fighting temptation was kept to a minimum.

Like all Sziverian government buildings, a monolithic cement structure housed the Records Department. Inside, a flurry of activity and crowd noises filled the building. Bella wound them through the mass of hurry-up-and-wait, taking them to the proper line for inquiries, which was considerably shorter than the filing and duplicate lines. At the counter, Markus held back and let her handle the official. Moments later, a stack of records was slid across, and they were directed to desks with privacy screens for viewing. They'd get an hour with the documents.

Unshouldering his pack, he used his foot to pull out both seats and sat. "I'll take half, you take half. Write down the establishment names and the owners. We can compare the lists at home."

Bella set the files down and sat beside him. "I hope an hour is enough time."

"We can return tomorrow if not."

The hour passed quicker than he anticipated, and when the official arrived to gather the files, Markus held up a finger and wrote the last two down while Bella scribbled her final observation. They both sagged in their chairs once left with nothing more than their notes.

Bella flexed her hand and grimaced. "I don't think I'll be able to write for the rest of the evening."

"At least we won't have to return to this chaos," he said, closing his notebook.

She drummed her fingers on her notes. "You were right about there only being a handful of owners. I noticed seven prominent hotel owners and nine prominent curtain show house owners. There were a few small inns that met the requirements for a business record by one or two rooms, but the actual hotels are run by either the same family or individual."

"We'll have to see who owns both," he said, rising. "And who hasn't suffered any losses."

CHAPTER

FIVE

EXHAUSTED AND IRRITATED, BELLA STUMBLED FROM bed, careful not to disturb the mattress and awaken Markus, who'd finally fallen asleep two hours ago. Halfway through the night, she'd almost given in and told him to sleep wherever he wanted. But how were they supposed to learn how to handle her ovulation phase if they didn't actually *handle* anything?

She took a moment to appreciate his masculine form sprawled across the large bed on his stomach. In nothing more than sleep pants, the cotton rode up one exposed leg to his knee, the stunning wolf tattoo on his back on full display. The contours of his muscles added depth and textures to the art, rose vines twisting and tangled, morphing into a wolf. Bella flexed her shoulders. A replica graced her back. Visual proof of her mating, an imprint that had somehow transferred from him to her the moment their bond fully forged.

His long, dark hair draped over his shoulders, across his pillow, and pooled on the sheets around him. Stars above, he was beautiful. She tethered her reaction to him before the sensation of her appreciation, which always turned into arousal, could awake him. Looking away, she reached for her robe tossed over the ottoman at the foot of the bed. She slid the cool bamboo silk blend over her arms. The thin material was only suitable for two months of the year, July and August, when the temperatures were warm enough not to need a fire at night.

Lunah stared at her through the screen sliding door left partially exposed all night, allowing for a fresh night breeze. Bella opened the partition. Lunah squeezed through and went straight to their bed, jumping onto the mattress and curling into Markus's side. He sighed and threw an arm around her. She dropped her muzzle on his back, her tail thumping loudly on the mattress.

While the wolf wasn't normally allowed on their bed, things were emotional enough for her to take her place at her alpha's side. Bella would not come between the need for the connection.

Bella left the door open sufficiently for Lunah to come and go from the room as she wished and went to the kitchen. The soft clink of porcelain sounded.

Madeleine glanced up from pouring tea and smiled. "Good morning, daughter mine. Tea?"

"Coffee?" Bella asked, covering a sudden yawn.

Laughing, her mother set the kettle on the cast iron stove and reached for the coffee jar. "Any food?"

Bella plopped onto a barstool at the huge island that ran the length of the kitchen. She dropped her head into her hands. "Probably."

Madeleine made an uh-oh noise. "Trouble?"

Discussing her sex life— or lack of at the moment— with her mother wasn't going to happen. Bella dragged a bowl of fruit closer and rolled apples and pears around. "Just fig- uring things out."

"I don't think couples ever stop trying to figure things out," Madeleine chuckled. "Two unique individuals are thrown into a shared life, troubles are sure to arise."

Glass and metal clinked as Madeleine set the kettle and a pan on the stove. A soft laugh left her again. "I remember this time with your father, oh, I was so mad at him over something so stupid when I think about it now. At the time? I couldn't even stand to look at Davis."

Bella propped her chin on her hand. "What did father do?"

Madeleine pulled flour and sugar from the cupboard to her right, setting them on the counter beside the stove. "He brought home all the wrong items from the store. I'd given him a very simple list before he left for work, and he must have forgotten it or lost it at some point in the day because he came home with, well, nothing I'd asked for. I ended up bundling all three of you into the wagon cart and walking to the nearest shop myself."

"Why didn't you leave us at home with him?"

Madeleine glanced over her shoulder, smiling. "That's how mad I was. I couldn't even think. I was so used to carting you three around I packed you all up out of habit. Likewise, your father was too frustrated to point out he could watch you kids. It was a mess all around."

The gentle crack of eggshells breaking against the rim of a bowl sounded. Madeleine tossed the empty shells into the sink. "When I returned home, dinner was waiting on the table, where your poor father sat, so exhausted he'd fallen asleep. Davis had tried to take some of the burden of caring for the family onto himself and, in the process, had reached his limits. I didn't know what to do except be thankful and try to be more understanding the next time he made a mistake. And now? Well, you know I'd take the wrong items every time I asked if I had him back."

"I miss him," Bella whispered.

She often wondered what her father would have thought of Markus. Of having a powerful Ruthenian beast master having left everything behind for her to become a part of their family. Bella couldn't imagine *his* family was happy with the decision. He never spoke of them, other than a cousin who could draw. So far, no one had written or even radioed. Did he miss them?

As if Madeleine had read Bella's mind, she said, "I wish he could have met Markus."

"Do you think he would have liked him?" Bella asked, tracing a wood knot on the polished counter.

"More than he'd have liked his other two children-in-laws," she said dryly. "Your husband doesn't shy away from the difficult."

Bella offered a weak smile. "No, he doesn't."

Unless the difficult situation involved the chance of getting pregnant, then he shied far, far away. She sighed. No, that wasn't fair. Last night, he'd stuck by her side despite the obvious distress being near her had caused. He hadn't left or even complained. Bella twisted on the stool and glanced at the opening to the short hall that led to their room. The urge to return to his side had her touching a toe to the floor.

She wasn't the only one needing to be together.

Markus staggered to the wide archway, leaned a forearm on the wall, and inhaled the rising scent of coffee and whatever sweet thing her mother was making. Pancakes stuffed with peaches, if Bella had to guess. His hair was a glorious mess around his face, falling to the center of his bare chest.

Morning light revealed all the lovely angles

of his very fit physique. From the ridges of his stomach muscles to the harsh cut of his hips and the delicious sprinkling of chest hair that condensed into a single line leading straight to his... She raised a brow and bit her lip. A tendril of lust shot right to her core. She lifted her gaze to his, where he watched her with a predatory intensity. Not helpful. He made to walk to her, and she shook her head.

Pausing mid-step, he stared at her in confusion. Bella pointed at him and then behind herself. He shrugged. She resisted the urge to smack her forehead. Sliding off the barstool, she rushed to meet him before he embarrassed himself.

She rose on her tiptoes and gave him a quick kiss, reaching between them to touch the erection straining against the thin fabric of his sleep pants. "I didn't think you wanted my mother to see this," she whispered against his lips.

He groaned and dropped his head back. "*Zhak'tu.*"

"I can—"

"*Vye,*" he hissed, taking a step back.

Bella dropped her hand with a sharp stab of disappointment. Squeezing his eyes closed, he blindly reached for her. Bella took hold of his hand, wanting to press it to her chest, where her heart raced. He pulled her into the privacy of the hall.

"If I let you touch me, I will be buried so far inside of you we will give new meaning to the term becoming one," he growled lowly. "Just... let me handle the problem. I'll be back out in a few moments."

She wanted to argue they were adults who could control themselves. Except... for the nearly three months they'd been married, they *hadn't* managed to touch without taking things to the inevitable conclusion. Even after they'd both brought each other to pleasure, they still needed more. Markus had argued such yesterday he still seemed determined to keep their contact to simple touches and kisses alone. Bella squeezed his hand and kissed his cheek.

"All right," she said and released his fingers.

The golden of his irises nearly glowed when he finally opened his eyes. He brushed his fingers along her jaw to the pulse fluttering at her throat. "So beautiful."

Bella stayed rooted in place. If he dragged her into the room with him, she wouldn't resist or complain. He swallowed and stepped back, a tremor racing his whole form, sweat glistening faintly on his skin. Sexual need pulsed through her body with enough force to tighten her inner muscles. His hand fell, and he turned on his heel fast enough to send his hair flying. Bella curled her toes into the cold wood to keep from running after him.

Two more days. They only had to make it through two more days. Closing her eyes, she inhaled to try to release some of the tension. Only an orgasm or five would eliminate all the built-up strain. Maybe later, she'd take a page from his method of coping and take care of herself.

She returned to her stool, thankful to find a steaming cup of coffee prepared the way she preferred. Rich cream sweetened with vanilla sugar. She took a small taste and groaned. "Thank you."

"You're welcome." Madeleine peered at the empty hall. "I thought I noticed Markus?"

"He's going to take a quick shower," Bella said, hoping her frustration and longing were hidden behind her slurp from the cup.

"Hopefully, he won't be too long," Madeleine said, removing a pancake from the pan. "I don't want his breakfast to get cold."

Bella smiled and took another sip.

"I INSTRUCTED the driver to let us off at the corner instead of in front of the business," Markus said, perching on the edge of the bench seat as they came to a slow stop.

"Why?" Bella asked, brows raised.

"There are two beast masters in this city. Myself, and one of the most powerful men in the nation. I don't want to be responsible for excessive speculation."

Not that Markus wouldn't enjoy the arch guardian of Wolvenguard having to attempt to explain what he was doing at a curtain show house. However, drawing that level of attention to the case would likely send the arsonist running. Markus didn't have time to chase a firebug.

Bella petted between Lunah's ears. "Should we have left her behind?"

"No, we left her behind yesterday. I doubt anyone will tell us where she's concerned at the hotels or the curtain show houses." The door swung open, sending air the perfect temperature rushing inside.

Lunah jumped out first. Markus followed and then helped Bella down. After paying the driver, he motioned to the left.

"This curtain show is owned by who again?" Bella asked.

"A Mr. Emler, he only owns this establishment, but he sold the building Mr. Weldon put across the street from Roane's Entertainment or whatever when he fell behind on payments."

Bella laughed. "Roane's Enjoyment Entertainment."

"Right. Following the theory that Mr. Weldon may be being targeted, perhaps Roane and this guy have a mutual grudge. But I'm not entirely convinced. None of the other fires were in businesses owned by more than one owner. They seem to be random." A navy banner with sparkling gold letters caught Markus's attention. He pointed. "And I believe that's our destination. Midnight Meetings."

A small side lot overflowed with bicycles and a lone Ariot. The expensive canvas over a wood-frame vehicle, powered by a small magnetic engine, made Markus raise a brow. The bikes weren't junk either. Most were in decent condition with oversized wheels for navigating in the colder weather, arriving in the coming months.

Bella paused at the parking area and looked around the street. "I'd expect this level of clientele near Extilis Square, but near The Rows?"

"There are three curtain show houses in this vicinity. One had a bad enough fire to shut down. We'll walk by after we're done here."

Bella rechecked her notebook. "That would be Silk Drapes Lounge."

"Yes."

A page turned. "Did you want to stop by Paradise Stage as well?"

"We'll see. I want to visit the fire sites near here, too."

He didn't think being exposed to repeated sexual situations would help them at the moment. Even now, he struggled not to haul her into the shallow privacy between two buildings and see how far she'd let him take her. Knowing his mate, all the way. And didn't that make things worse for him? Her sweet scent was so much *more* during her ovulation phase. A natural aphrodisiac that drove him to the brink and, if he allowed, would tip him over. The shower before breakfast and the private time he'd forced himself to take before they'd left had barely contained his need.

"There are two hotels near here, but," she turned and pointed, "two blocks that way is another curtain show house and hotel. According to their addresses, they're practically the same building. One is 620A, and the other is 620B for street numbers."

He chanced leaning closer to view her notes. "Neither has experienced a fire?"

"No."

"Does the same person own both?"

Bella turned the page and laughed. She pointed.

Markus turned his head enough to meet her amused stare. "Guess that was the property Weldon outbid Burnsean on."

She smiled, pressed a quick kiss to his lips, and flounced away before he could react. Lunah trotted after Bella. The fluffy length of the wolf's tail swung in apparent contentment to be out with her people. Markus grasped the strap to his pack, squared his shoulders, and followed them.

Inside, lush navy velvet curtains draped over navy velvet damask golden wallpaper. Yellow flames burned behind red glass, muting the light. A little bell tinkered as the solid wood plank door closed firmly behind them. Plush golden carpet soaked up their footsteps. Two candlesticks burned on either side of an open book, where a red feather fountain pen lay.

"I wonder if they all have sign-in logs," Bella said, tapping her finger on the paper.

A woman pushed a curtain aside behind the desk. Pale blonde curls gleamed atop her head in the low light. Pink, cream and gray sheer strips of fabric crisscrossed over her torso and fell in ribbons to the floor. With each step, the material moved, revealing a different glimpse of her nude flesh beneath. Round hips. Soft stomach. Breasts small enough to not need support but large enough to entice men who preferred their women endowed with more than a handful. For the representation of the carnality to be discovered within the establishment, the woman was an admirable choice.

She looked between them, a sensual smile playing on her glossy lips. "Afternoon, welcome to Midnight Meetings. Will today's visit be for one showroom or two?"

"Neither," Markus answered, his touch seeking his mate before he could realize what he was doing. His hand gripped her hip, pulling her against his body. "We just have some questions."

The woman reached beneath the counter and removed a folded pamphlet. Her gaze locked on Markus, and she shifted her torso, a sheer band of fabric sliding enough to reveal a soft pink nipple. "Absolutely, I love answering questions. Many people are curious about what happens here. We do offer a comprehensive guide, which you're free to take with you today."

"So polite," Bella murmured.

The woman pushed the brochure across the counter with one finger. "We do aim to please. What questions may I answer?"

"Have you heard about the fires at other curtain show houses in the city?" Bella asked.

"What is your name?" Markus asked when the woman stared at them.

"M-my name?" she asked, touching a hand to her chest, displacing the already precarious fabric to expose one pale breast fully.

"Does no one ever ask you that?" Bella asked, her fingers curling in the air as if she wanted to reach across the space and cover the woman's breast.

"Sure, they do. I mean, they want to know all the entertainer's names, so if they like our look, they can choose a room to view us in. I was just confused since you're wondering about fires. I had nothing to do with any fires," she said quickly, sliding her fingers up the gauzy fabric strips to the shoulder to adjust the strips over her exposed chest.

"We aren't accusing you of anything," Bella assured. "We're just wondering what you may have heard."

"Are you with the paper or something? Mr. Emler said to direct all inquiries to him. I can," she reached under the counter again, "give you his card."

"A card would be great," Markus said, accepting the small white stationery. "Your name would also be great. We're not with the paper."

Bella poised the fountain pen above her notebook. "We're investigating the fires."

The woman's fingers fluttered at the

shoulder straps again. "Like, with HCES? The papers said the fires are all accidental."

"We're not with HCES."

"Oh, good," she breathed, letting loose a breathy laugh. "Mr. Emler doesn't like them either."

Bella raised a brow. "Oh?"

"I mean, oh shoot, that sounds bad, doesn't it? Okay, look, Mr. Emler is a very private man. And this place?" She lifted her hands. "This is his baby. He doesn't want any trouble."

"We don't want any trouble, either," Markus assured her, wondering what it would take to get a name out of her. "We want to make sure nothing sinister is happening."

"And you need to know who you talk to," she said, nodding. "Yes, I understand. I'm Larena. I work two shifts, three days a week. First shift up here and second shift in a viewing room. I'm always in room seven, in case you want to watch."

"Do a lot of employees work double shifts?" Bella asked.

"Most of us do, so we can get more hours with less work. But some of the performers only like to work the rooms. You can sometimes make more doing that," Larena answered, twisting a strip of fabric between her fingers near her waist.

"Do performers change show houses often?" Markus asked.

Larena shook her head. "No, because we get a client base where we work. I've only known two people who left here or came here from another house, and that was because they had an issue with a client getting too fixated." She glanced around and then leaned forward. "It's a risk we take."

Markus imagined there was a fine line between loyalty and obsession in this industry. "Do fanatical patrons often cause trouble?"

"No, not that I've ever heard. Once you relocate, they don't come searching for you, thankfully."

The pen nub scratched as Bella made notes. "And there aren't any other issues between clients and performers?"

"Most people don't like interacting with anyone while they're here. They enjoy the anonymity we provide on both sides of the curtain. I don't know them personally, and they don't know anything about me other than my name. Mr. Elmer has rules about engaging with patrons."

"And everyone follows the rules?" Markus asked.

"They do if they want to continue working here," a new voice added.

A woman with cropped black hair and alabaster skin in a short, low-cut black beaded gown pushed through the curtain. Bright red lipstick drew attention to her full lips, while smoky eyeshadow brought mystery to her dark eyes. Where Larena was meant to entice, this woman fit with the elegant interior.

"Your stage rooms are full," the woman

said. "I'm here to take over welcoming for you."

Larena gasped. "So early?" She gathered the length of ribbons into both her hands. "I wish you luck in your investigation."

Markus glanced around, noting the opening to a corridor. "Is there another entrance?"

"Only for pass holders." She laid her hands on the countertop. "I'm Willow. May I continue to assist you this afternoon?"

"We were asking Larena questions about the fires at other curtain show houses," Bella answered.

Willow folded her arms on the counter and leaned forward, drawing further attention to her ample breasts. "My husband was telling me about the fires. He had some concerns as well. He works for the SNID."

Markus carefully schooled his features. He couldn't compare his relationship with Bella to anyone else's. Theirs was completely unique. And if anyone saw his wife in a state of undress the way he did, he'd have to pop their eyes from their skull. Bella rubbed a soothing hand along his forearm. Lunah nudged his thigh. The performer didn't stare at him in horror, so he must have succeeded in keeping his abhorrence private.

"Who is he?" Bella asked. "I used to work there."

"Cedar Moonberry," Willow answered,

smiling. "I think those at the building know him as C.G.?"

C.G.'s name was Cedar? Markus coughed away his laughter. Bella dug her elbow into his side.

"I know C.G. I worked as a guardian's assistant and then in long storage for a time," Bella said.

Willow's eyes widened, and her smile grew. "You must be Ella! He was so disappointed when you left. He said you were very organized and easy to work with."

"Bella," his mate corrected. "How long have you been contracted?"

Willow's smile faltered a bit. "Ten months."

Markus recalled C.G.'s rule about one-year contracts with the same woman only once. But, the SNID employee's love life wasn't the main interest. "What concerned C.G. about the fires?"

Willow straightened and pulled up the top of her dress. "That there were so many for one type of business. The industry I happen to work for. It made him nervous."

Bella glanced over her shoulder at him, her brows raised, her curiosity flaring across their bond. Indeed. Perhaps the beautiful Willow had managed to do what the others before her couldn't, convince C.G. a long-term marriage was worth the risk.

"Did he say if the SNID will be investigating?" Markus asked.

Willow shook her head. "I think he tried to mention it to someone, but..." She shrugged. "I guess it was as important to them as it was to HCES. No one believes it's anything except accidental."

"What do you think?" Bella asked.

Willow smoothed her hands over the dark, polished wood. "I think this business can lead to some jealousy between lovers, and I also think it creates a false sense of intimacy to the viewers that, if not returned, can cause some anger."

"Larena told us if there's an issue with a patron, performers will change venues, and that usually solves issues," Bella said.

"Yes, and I agree that usually does work with an infatuated viewer."

"But maybe not this time," Markus surmised.

"Perhaps not this time," Willow agreed. "I only know performers at two of the houses that experienced the fires."

"Did they have customers they were worried about?" Bella asked, her muscles tensing beneath his touch.

"One of them did, yes," Willow said slowly. "I can give you her information if you'd like."

"That'd be great," Bella said, turning her notebook to face Willow. "Have you had any suspicious customers here at Midnight Meetings?"

"No one that jumps out at me, no," Willow said, scribbling words onto the paper. "Most of our clients are single, lonely, keep-to-them-selves types. Not even the sex hustlers who work down the street can entice them once they leave here. They walk in with limited words and leave the same. One of the reasons I love working here. I can do my show and not worry about anyone propositioning me for more."

"That's common? The propositions and sex hustlers outside establishments?" Markus asked.

"Outside here, yes. Other places? Some of them allow workers inside. In secret, of course, because if the HCES found out, they'd be shut down so fast the curtains wouldn't even have a chance to fall. Mr. Emler has informed the HCES of the workers near here in hopes they clear them out. He said he doesn't need a human rabies syndrome episode ruining his business."

"Wise man," Markus said.

Willow pressed a hand to her stomach. "Absolutely."

The bell on the door tinkered. Markus and Bella stepped back from the counter. A woman with a large hat and a gown buttoned up to her chin went to the counter, signed the book, and disappeared through the opening to the corridor beyond.

Willow smiled. "She is our typical customer. Once they learn who they prefer, they sign in and go straight to an open showroom. Those whom Mr. Emler has vetted can secure a pass for a fee and not sign in, just put one of their allotted tickets into a box so he knows they've been here."

"You've been very helpful, thank you," Bella said, picking up her notebook. "If we have any more questions, can we talk to you?"

"Absolutely, and if you ever want to be shown around, we have several rooms designated for couples," Willow said, smiling a different sort of smile than the others she'd offered. "You may find the experience most stimulating."

Bella snorted. "Trust me, we don't need help in that department."

CHAPTER

SIX

Staring up at the imposing gray stone building rising seven stories into the air, Bella took a deep breath. She didn't think she'd ever have to enter the Sziverian National Investigative Division again, which was silly. She'd married a Ruthenian investigator, whom she'd met in this very building. Anything larger than local enforcement services could handle nationwide landed on the desk of an SNID guardian, such as her former boss.

The weight of Markus's hand slid along her hip. "Come on, the doors won't be open for much longer."

The workday was ending. The summer months allowed for the guardians to work until eight, a tradeoff for when they couldn't work at all during the winter. The warm glow of sunset kissed the horizon, a subtle countdown to the approaching night and the closing of official buildings. They'd eaten and then visited the nearby fire sites before coming here to speak with C.G.

Only one of the buildings had burned completely. The other two were still functioning and either in the process of or had been, repaired. The employees had little to say other than where the fire had started, most in accessible areas to any guest. The dining room, game rooms, or corridors outside of visitor accommodations. Untraceable to the clientele of either business. Whoever they were dealing with knew how to remain anonymous in their crime. A frustrating development.

Bella squared her shoulders and took the wide steps to the line of doors. People entered and exited, some with documents, folders, or briefcases, others with nothing. All in a rush. Inside, the cavernous lobby bustled with activity. Bella ignored the sign-in desk, heading to the basement door on the left. Lunah's claws clicked on the tile floor behind her.

Their steps echoed on the cement stairs to the corridors below. Room after room lined the halls, each labeled with numbers and nothing more. If someone didn't know where to go, they'd get lost in the maze of interrogation, storage, and utility rooms. Bella had worked in the dank, underground level. She knew where evidence short and long storage were both located.

Lanterns spaced every twenty feet provided just enough light to see. Lunah ambled at her side, brushing against her thigh and hip. Bella sank her fingers into the soft fur between the wolf's shoulders, allowing some of the day's tension to leave her. Not only did she know where evidence was located, but she also knew where the empty storage rooms were. The ones guaranteed to offer privacy. More than one guardian in the building had made use of them.

The constant companion of Markus's need frayed her nerves and made every step difficult. She *ached*. Part of her wanted to beg him to tether their bond, understanding why he'd made the choice. The other was thankful he continued to trust her to share in his misery. An aggressive desire to know if an orgasm from her would sate the lust on his end had her flexing her fingers. Because what he'd done for himself had made little difference. Squeezing her eyes closed, she reigned in her wayward thoughts. Again.

If she were to yank him into one of the empty rooms they walked by, release his erection from his pants, and fall to her knees, giving him little choice, he'd let her. And then, after, he'd be ashamed, convinced his need for release somehow outweighed her need to give it to him, making him a selfish lover. Only twice had she managed to get her greedy hands on him in such a manner. Never her mouth. She'd read enough, seen enough art, to know men wanted, craved, that act. Somehow, Bella had to figure out how to convince her husband she *wanted* to bring him pleasure because it was what she alone desired.

Not in the basement of the SNID, however.

Fisting Lunah's fur between her fingers, Bella opened her eyes and took a corridor branch to the right. The faint glow from the short-term storage's open door gave her something else to focus on. No one stood at the narrow counter, a chain-link fence separating the compact waiting area from the spacious evidence room. A flicker of light deep within the shadowy room showed her where C.G. worked. Bella tapped a bell and then drummed her fingers on the wood surface.

"Give me a second!" a male voice echoed.

"One," Markus whispered into her ear.

A shiver raced up her spine. She couldn't help the sudden flare of desire. Turning her head, she discovered his mouth, only a breath from hers. Without a second thought, Bella pressed her lips to his, her tongue probing for entrance. Groaning, he opened, the hot length of his tongue gliding along hers. Bella turned enough to wrap her arms around his broad shoulders. His hands sought out her hips, burrowing under her shirt to find her bare skin.

Sparks of awareness tingled where his fingers brushed, something that hadn't changed since the first time he'd touched her. She arched into him, her hands grasping the fabric of his shirt for leverage. If she rose on her tiptoes just a little, she'd manage to get the hard length pressing into her belly... oh *yes*. Right there. Unashamed, she tilted her pelvis, opened one of her thighs, and rocked against his erection. He deepened the kiss, angling his head, his mouth devouring her, his tongue doing all sorts of wicked things, setting her already heated blood completely on fire.

Embarrassing as the situation might be, Bella realized she was in danger of orgasming, and she couldn't even care. She needed the release. They both did. Maybe she should have dragged him into an unlocked room after all. Their little make-out session wasn't exactly private. But he didn't seem to care about their very public display of affection, either. He pulled her tighter against him, his hips meeting hers, adding to the erotic bursts of pleasure gathering at her core.

"Oh! I had heard you'd married. Hello, Bella," C.G. said behind them. Something clanged, and he made a harried exclamation.

Markus tore his mouth free, his breath a heavy rush across her damp lips. "Damn it," he growled.

His hands dug deeper into her hips before releasing her. Frustration zipped across their bond, whether from the interruption or how quickly they'd ignited into passion, she didn't know. Bella ground her teeth together, squeezed her eyes closed for patience for a second and spun around, forcing all semblance of latent need and unspent desire from her features.

She smiled at C.G., bracing a forearm on

the counter. "Hello, C.G. We met your most recent wife today, too."

C.G. stood, a metal tube in one hand and disorganized papers in the other. "Willow? How did you meet her?"

"A Mr. Weldon hired us to investigate the fires at his curtain show houses and hotels."

"Ah. Yes. Those fires are alarming. I hadn't realized hotels were affected as well." The tube rang as he set it down on top of the papers. "I'm not certain what's going on, but I don't think there's anything accidental about them."

"We agree," Markus answered. "Has anyone thought to open an investigation?"

C.G. shook his head. "No. There's only been two other suspected arsonists since I've worked here, and neither was caught. The division feels it's a waste of resources to investigate them now when only property is damaged. If the business owner can come up with conclusive evidence, then accusations can be leveled, but otherwise, until someone is injured or killed, authorities won't get involved."

Defeat made Bella's shoulders sag. "So, there's nothing?"

C.G. glanced at the open door to his space. "I wouldn't say that, exactly."

Bella leaned forward. "What do you mean?"

Once again, C.G.'s gaze darted to the doorway.

Markus sighed. "Lunah, *custrazva*," he said. Lunah's claws clicked on the cement floor.

"There," her husband huffed. "She is guarding the hall and will let us know if anyone is coming. Speak."

"All right, look, this needs to stay between us, okay?" C.G. said softly. "I pursued an Incorva a couple of years ago. The whole family are scene artists. Things didn't work out between us. She wanted five years and an attempt to start a family. You know—"

Bella waved her hand. "Yes, yes, I know. Completely against your standards. One year. One woman. On to the next."

C.G.'s head bounced in the affirmative. "Right. Well, we did get along great, and we've remained friends. I asked her to do a huge favor and document the burn sites for the curtain show houses. I didn't know about the hotels, or I would have asked her to do those, too."

"And your Willow does not know about this woman," Markus said, his hand sliding around to rest on Bella's hip.

C.G. blinked and jerked his head back, light reflecting off his glasses. "M-my Willow? My... no, I mean, I haven't introduced them. She doesn't have anything to worry about, though. Jeanie is happily married with two kids now. Like I said, we're just friends."

"Then why keep her a secret from your wife?" Markus asked. Bella nudged him. They needed C.G.'s cooperation, not his anger.

"Willow is..." C.G. dug his fingers through his mop of dark hair. "She's a Faneline and not as secure with me as I'd hoped. I mean, I almost didn't contract with her because, you know."

Disappointed, Bella frowned at the man. Yes, she knew. Faneline's were true orphans. They couldn't pass on the name to a spouse or a child. If Willow ever had a baby out of wedlock, a rarity in Sziveria, she'd have to give the child the father's first name if he didn't do the honorable thing and contract with her. Most Fanelines ended up in jobs precisely like the one Willow had found herself in, or worse. How many men had dangled the promise of their name in front of her like C.G.?

"She's a beautiful woman. Did you allow her to take your family name?" Bella asked.

"If she wanted, she could have. You know I have no control over that," C.G. answered. "But she said Moonberry wouldn't be any different than Faneline if I, that is if we, only committed to one year. The name still wouldn't be hers."

How depressing. "And still no longer than a year, hmm?"

C.G.'s gaze went hazy. "I don't know, she's... different. In so many ways. I'm... wow, I can't believe I'm saying this out loud, but yes, I'm considering asking her for longer. She has this plan for her future, and it didn't include me, still doesn't unless I want it to, and it's incredibly tempting."

"Who knew all a woman had to do was get you to imagine her lifelong plans that didn't involve you," Bella teased.

His blue eyes widened, and he held open his hands. "Right? Crazy. But there it is. I really like her, though."

"That's good. You should at least like the person you plan to be married to. Did you meet her at the curtain show?"

"No, she has a firm rule about dating viewers. We met at a coffee shop if you can believe that," he said, a wry grin turning his lips. "I would go on my way to work; she would go after her shift was over. We met waiting in line."

"And you don't mind her job?" Markus asked.

C.G. shook his head. "No. There's a wall of glass between her and the viewers. She can't even see them. It's one way. She took me in once to show me how it works." He blushed. "She gave me a private show. Explained to me while she was working what she had to do to make sure patrons continued putting in raimarks to keep the curtains up. It's a job for her, nothing more."

Now Bella was curious. She hadn't been before, but she wondered what lengths a performer went to keep their audience engaged enough to continue paying money to watch until the end. Wondered if she'd be fascinated or appalled, or perhaps a mixture of both.

"What did your friend, the scene artist, have to say?" Markus asked, interrupting her musings. As always, he kept them on track.

C.G. held up a finger while digging around

underneath the counter. He held up a large manila envelope. "I have all the scene sketches here. The last one, The Enchanting Stage, Jeanie was able to sketch while it still burned."

Bella's fingers twitched to get her hands on those drawings. "Why did you ask her to do them?"

"After the third fire, I was worried. If, at any point, another one led to a death in the future, I wanted the division to have a head start on the investigation. Willow works at these places, and the fires seem completely random." C.G. slid the envelope through the opening. "As I said earlier, I like my wife. I care a great deal for her. I want her to be safe."

Bella pulled the evidence closer. "Thank you for this."

"You'll keep me informed?"

She nodded. "Yes, and if Willow thinks of anything helpful, please let us know. We live at the new apartments over by Extilis Square."

C.G.'s brows shot up. "The Garden Building?"

"That's the one. We're in apartment 7C."

"Willow is saving to buy an apartment there, on the second level. She said it's the nicest apartment building in the entire city, and she'll be the only owner of her unit."

Bella smiled. "That's a lovely goal."

And she wanted the beautiful entertainer to be healthy and well enough to achieve her dreams. She clutched the envelope, the only solid evidence they had. Time wasn't on their side. If the conclusion they'd come to yesterday was correct, another fire would be set in two days. They needed to make sure it wasn't where the lovely Willow performed.

ALONE IN THE BEDROOM, Bella sat on the hardwood floor surrounded by drawings of charred walls and furniture. Markus and Lunah had gone for a run, either in the greenhouse or along the quiet city blocks. The sun had set long ago, and the night was a balmy fifty. A calm breeze from the screened sunroom fluttered her hair and teased the pages on the floor.

After they'd left the SNID, they'd returned home and eaten dinner. Markus had been tense, a strain he'd tried to hide from her mother but couldn't keep from Bella. After they finished eating and he helped with the dishes, he and Lunah had left. Not wanting to sit around and dwell on the growing pressure between them, she'd collected C.G.'s drawings and disappeared into their room. The big, empty bed seemed to mock her, so she'd put her back on the piece of furniture and lost herself in crime scenes.

Bella started with the first fire, The Sizzle Show. The destruction was complete. By the time Jeanie Incorva had sketched the scene, all that remained were burnt support beams, door frames, and piles of ash. How everyone had evacuated before the entire place interrupted into an inferno, Bella didn't know.

Closing her eyes, she touched the page and allowed herself to be tugged into the image. The shift into a new space was subtle, a sensation of reality altering, of black pencil sketches on white paper becoming her new existence. In her psyche, Bella opened her eyes and moved around the ruins. The curtain show house had been a single story with two wings stretching at an angle from a lobby. Remnants of a desk, a large clay pot, and the back of a chair were all that remained of the gathering space.

Moving her fingers to the next page, Bella walked to the right wing, peering through a doorframe. The doorknob lay among the ash within the room. Nothing else appeared to have survived, or Jeanie didn't bother to draw. Bella's fingers never left the paper as she moved to the other side of the building. Here, not even frames or furniture remained, the fire having burned hotter. Bella would bet this was where the arsonist started the blaze.

Dragging herself from the scene, she took a moment to reacclimate to the bedroom before reaching for her notebook. She jotted down a few notes and then moved on to the next establishment, Velvet and Candlelight. Another single-story building with spacious viewing rooms from what she could tell. A few broken bits of furniture dotted the scene but otherwise didn't give her much to work on.

The scene sketches from Velvet and Candlelight gave her a better glimpse of how the houses were arranged. The fire had decimated the showroom nearby, but the rest of the building remained functional. Broken glass glittered among the ash. Charred sections of curtains slumped over a risen square stage, which twelve rooms were arranged around, the largest rooms being corner rooms.

Jeanie had drawn a perspective from two rooms, a smaller straight-on view, and a larger corner view. The entire corner section of the viewing area was glass, and Bella wondered how much more it cost the patron to have the curtain remain open. The corner across from Bella in the sketch was completely burnt, whereas the room Bella stood within still had a frame, though the glass had shattered, and the curtains had burned.

The other drawings of Terrance Weldon's property, Sultry Glass Show and Drink offered similar sights. The most recent fire, The Enchanting Stage, had been captured while a fire still burned, as C.G. had promised. Bella spent extra time on the scene, looking over the faces of those gathered to watch a fire and those who helped extinguish the flames licking out into the night.

"Find anything interesting?" Markus's voice whispered into the charcoal drawn night.

Bella's first instinct was to withdraw from her private world, but cowardly, she wasn't ready to deal with the unbearable sensual hunger just looking at him caused. She slid her fingers to the next drawing. Jeanie had been allowed inside after the fire was doused.

"All of the fires started in or near a viewer room, so I think a patron is to blame," she said, taking in the scorched walls of a corridor. Flames had kissed the inside of two rooms but hadn't extended beyond.

"They keep logs. Maybe someone was able to grab the sign-ins before they burned."

"Or we'll just need to research from the buildings that didn't have any damage to that part of the business."

A touch ghosted from her shoulder to her wrist, stopping shy of her hand. "Come out, Bella," he whispered into her ear.

Her fingers pressed harder to the paper a second before she broke contact. Bright, golden eyes stared into hers the moment her eyelids fluttered open. Lunah licked her nose before padding away, disappearing through the open door to the sunroom-converted greenhouse. Bella loved the feature, which had to have been expensive. The glass panels would be replaced when the temperatures dropped heading into autumn.

Bella had expected Markus. He'd been touching her after all, hadn't he? Twisting around, she found him leaning against the bathroom door, his hair wet, his shirt and pants unbuttoned as if he'd just dragged them on. He looked... delicious. She quickly looked away, focusing on the papers in front of her.

"Enjoy your run?" she asked, gathering the

pages together in the order she'd need them again if she had to revisit the scenes.

"It was necessary," he said softly. "Lunah needed to expel energy being here all day and again tonight. I needed... the same."

She bit her lip to keep from shouting if he'd only allow her to touch him, *maybe* he wouldn't need to escape her presence. The *maybe* was what kept her silent. While she wanted to touch him with a desperation that scared her, she didn't know if anything would change. She knew the forced celibacy was only making everything worse. His being forbidden intensified her need. Made her grumpy.

"I want to go to the curtain show houses tonight when they're at their busiest," he said, the wood floor groaning as he neared.

"Do you want to go to one that had a fire, or just choose one at random?"

"Where's the list?" he asked, buttoning his shirt. What a shame.

Bella forced her attention back to her task. "Living room table."

He disappeared through the door. The deep rumble of his voice and her mother's much lighter one drifted to her in incoherent syllables. Glancing at the bedside clock, she noted the hour neared ten. A quick check showed Jeanie had gone to the last fire around midnight. Hopping up with the paper in hand, she went into the living room.

Madeleine smiled and blew her a kiss goodnight before heading down the corridor opposite theirs to her room. Four rooms were located down the hall. The apartment was huge, taking up a quarter of the entire seventh floor. Someday, Markus would allow her ovulation phase to serve its purpose, and the rooms would be filled with little ones. The thought made her both nervous and excited.

Pushing thoughts of procreation from her mind, Bella held up the sketch. "The fire started before midnight at The Enchanting Stage."

Markus flipped a page in her notebook. "Then late nights are a good time to go."

"Yes. I wonder if we can learn when the other fires started if the owners can tell us."

"Would be helpful." He flipped the book around and tapped the page. "Let's try here, The Night Embrace."

She raised her brows. "The one next to Mr. Weldon's hotel?"

"Yes. He considers the owner of this curtain house a suspect. Let's see what we can learn."

CHAPTER
SEVEN

IF ONE MORE WOMAN JIGGLED HER BARE BUTT cheeks as she passed Markus, Bella would not be held responsible for what happened. The men and women who worked at The Night Embrace enticed viewers to their rooms by mingling among the clients between shows wearing very little. Corsets and thongs. Vests and tight briefs with padded crotches. The curtain show house created a mingling environment with an appetizer buffet and bar, treating the end of a show not as something finished but as an intermission. They'd arrived at such time.

The men had different standards than the women. They encouraged anyone who wished to touch anywhere they desired. When someone took them up on their offer, they'd whisper into their ear, leaving the person flushed. Bella spent a lot of time half-hidden behind Markus, not wanting to be approached.

No, thank you. Only one man interested her enough to fondle.

The women teased.

The men seduced.

Lust vibrated through the entire atmosphere.

Bella couldn't wait to leave.

So far, they'd learned Gerall Burnsean valued his customers to the point of mingling among them, showing off and praising the men and women who performed for the house. When a little bell rang, he even escorted several patrons to their room selections personally. Soon, only Bella, Markus, and a handful of others meandered around the spacious social room. Burnsean returned and headed straight to a short, thin man stacking his plate full of snack foods.

Markus tensed and pulled her back into the shadows near the wall, where a thick velvet brocade curtain sagged to the tile floor. The man turned, and Bella was the one tensing. Hossman. The man who'd held her father's debt before he'd died and had held her mother to his ridiculous interest rate for the loan. The reason they'd had to live in squalor in The Rows. The infernal little man popped a crusted something into his mouth, chewing with relish while Burnsean waited, rocking on his heels.

"Delicious. I wonder, how much does this little setup eat into your bottom line? If I'm going to be a partner in your ventures, I think I deserve to know," Hossman said, his words gravely and low. An orange, cream, and turquoise striped scarf wound around his neck. A short-sleeved white shirt showed off arms thin as pencils.

Gerral Burnsean lifted his chin and smoothed a hand down his slate gray vest. Like his performers, he wore no shirt underneath, though thankfully, a pair of expensive black silk blend pants covered his legs. "Every one of my curtain rooms is in use. I don't think other showhouses can say the same. I'm not interested in a partnership that will change my business model, know what I mean?"

Hossman waved a chunk of torn bread around. The bright lamp light suspended from the ceiling flashed off his glasses. "No, no, I just want to make sure my profits won't be spared for this feast."

"I assure you, your profits will not suffer," Gerall stated between clenched teeth.

A hunk of meat disappeared into Hossman's mouth. He chewed, gazing up at the glass lanterns suspended at different lengths from the ceiling. Once the bite was finished, he gave a dismissing toss of his hand. "You may go. I wish to look around at how the business runs when you aren't hovering around your employees."

Gerall's hands fisted as he offered a forced smile. "Of course. I will be in my office until the next intermission."

Hossman lifted a glass of something pale and sparkly. Champagne? The drink was imported from Italyssa and very expensive. "Have to keep those raimarks flowing, right?"

"Indeed." Gerall pivoted on his left foot and left.

Smacking noises left Hossman. His fingers wiggled over the variety of foods on his plate. Bella wondered what would drive a person to agree to do business with such a nasty man. She wanted to grab a roll from a basket near her and pitch it at his head. Even found her hand reaching for the buttery bread. Markus grasped her wrist and moved her arm back to her side. He gave a subtle head shake when she glanced up at him. Hossman left the room, muttering to himself. A tall, bulky man followed. His security, whom he'd made wait in the hall like a servant.

Bella clenched her jaw. "He didn't even notice us."

"I didn't want him to," Markus said quietly. His hand moved from her wrist to grasp her fingers. "Come on, let's see if we can find the owner's office."

Unpleasant thoughts swirled through Bella's mind. Her fingers squeezed Markus's. "It has to be him," she whispered. "Hossman must be starting the fires for Burnsean. Some kinds of a business deal."

"We shall see," Markus said, pulling her along as he turned down a long, unadorned corridor.

When had they left the room with the food? She blinked and looked around. Plain wood walls. Plain carpeted floor. A few sketches of beautiful women hanging on the walls with flower paintings. Lanterns on narrow tables. Bella wondered if they'd passed an employee's only sign. An open door at the end of the hall spilled light into the dim hall. Markus released her hand and stalked to the office.

Bella hurried after, not wanting to miss a moment or the explanation. Gerall Burnsean glanced up from a paper he'd been writing on when they set foot in his space. His pale gaze slid over Markus, then Bella. He licked his lips, heat flaring in his eyes.

He pointed the pen. "Yes. Absolutely." He motioned the pen in Bella's direction, his gaze sliding down her form again until she wanted to leave the room. "I mean, I usually like my women with larger assets. Some jiggle for the viewers, if you know what I mean. But with those legs?" He sucked his tongue against his teeth. "Again, absolutely. You may return to the welcome desk and tell Angelina I approve the request for an application."

Anger sliced a red-hot trail across their bond. *Oh no.* Bella tried to keep hold of Markus's hand, but he tore free, slammed his palms on the desk, and leaned forward. "You misunderstand my reason for standing in front of you, *durozak*."

Burnsean audibly swallowed, leaning back. The pen tumbled from his hand, rolled across the desk, and landed on the floor with a muted *thump*. Color drained from his complexion, leaving his already alabaster skin ghostly. She could only imagine the expression on her husband's face.

The man swallowed again, his Adam's apple bobbing. "Ruthenian. And she is—"

"My. Mate," Markus growled.

"Oh, stars above," he mewled, pressing back into his chair. "I didn't mean any disrespect. I get couples wanting to apply for jobs every single night. How was I to know you weren't interested?"

"Ask first, perhaps?" Markus said.

"Right, of course, you're so absolutely correct." Burnsean snapped his fingers and pointed at Markus with both hands. "Fantastic advice. I will be using it."

"What business do you have with Hossman?" Markus asked.

Burnsean pressed his mouth closed, his lips disappearing. He drummed his fingertips together. "Are you a competitor of his?"

"*Vye*."

Burnsean blinked. "Um."

"That means no," Bella offered. "We're investigating the hotel and curtain show house fires."

She didn't think it was prudent to mention they were hired by one of his rivals. The owner's gaze flickered in her direction again. Lingered. Markus shifted. Renewed irritation flared along their bond.

"Up here at me," Markus barked. "You do not get to look at her."

"Right, of course." Burnsean cleared his throat. "The fires. I don't know much about them other than several owners have had the unfortunate luck to have them."

"And you had nothing to do with that?" Markus asked, leaning forward. Bella inched to the left to peer around him.

Burnsean's eyelids flap-flapped. "What? No! Arctic, no, I've had nothing to do with that. Why in the inhabited world would I?"

"Increased business while eliminating competitors. Not that difficult to need a reason between owners," Markus stated.

The man pushed so far back in his seat that the frame groaned. "Man, oh come on, I love my industry. Fires are bad for all of us. They make people nervous, you know what I mean?"

"If you aren't starting fires, what interest do you have in partnering with Hossman?"

Burnsean licked his lips, holding up his hands. "Whoa, you have the wrong idea about the two of us, know what I mean?" He pressed a hand to the bare section of his skin above the vest. "I'm honest. I pay my taxes. I treat my employees with respect. I spoil my customers."

"You aren't answering the question," Markus said slowly.

With another swipe of his tongue across his lips, Burnsean held out his shaking palms. "All right, all right. I can see how, you know, my associating with a known crime boss might look a bit suspicious, all things considered. But, I swear, it has nothing to do with fires, other curtain shows houses or nothing like that. Swear."

"Why is it a secret?" Markus asked. "If it's not disreputable?"

"Look," Burnsean began, sliding both hands down the panels of his silk vest, "I'm a lover, not a challenger, you know what I mean?"

"*Vye,* explain it to me," Markus said, his accent thick.

"I tried to purchase the hotel sharing a block with my building, but I was outbid. I wasn't aggressive enough. I'm looking to expand. I want a show house and a hotel, side by side, and I'm determined to make it happen. A couple weeks ago, a property came on the market that would suit my purposes. It has what used to be a former restaurant, but with a little construction, it could easily be converted into a curtain show space. Mr. Hossman is going to help me acquire said property." He motioned his hands over the papers on the desk. "All on the level, like I said, I swear."

"What is he charging you to do this?"

Burnsean shrugged, opening a drawer. He pulled out a small box, flipped it open, and removed a thin paper-wrapped cigarette. He held the box out to Markus. "No?" The box snapped shut. "Best Miami Island has to offer."

Markus remained silent.

Clearing his throat, Burnsean leaned over

and used the nearest lamp to light the cigarette. A plume of sweet tobacco smoke drifted into the air. "If he can obtain the property for me, I've agreed to five percent for five years, plus a curtain room of his choice to remain private without an actual curtain."

"So free shows for five years in a room you can't profit from," Markus said.

Smoke blew from Burnsean's mouth and nose. "Yes. That was how I was able to get him down to the five percent profit shares." Cigarette balanced between two fingers, Bursean leaned forward. "I trust this will remain confidential. I don't need anyone else knowing my situation, know what I mean?"

"We're discrete and only share information pertinent to the crime if we have enough to take to authorities," Markus said, straightening from the desk. "Do you have any suspicions?"

The two spoke for a few minutes, Burnsean adding nothing new to the information they already had. Bella took notes anyway, figuring the more of the same they had, the more they could dismiss.

When they finished, Burnsean rose and snuffed out his cigarette but didn't offer his hand. "Would you like to partake in a show? On the house, I'll supply you with the proprietary coins to keep the curtain open."

Markus's hand slid along hers. "Perhaps another night. We have more places to visit before closing."

"Yes. Absolutely. Anything to make up for

the, you know," he waved a hand at them, "the misunderstanding. See my receptionist. She'll give you an hour's worth and an intermission room voucher."

They left the office, and Bella breathed in the clearer air of the hall. "What do you think?"

"I think we'll get the coins to have a reason to return," he said, guiding them along the route to return to the entrance.

Bella glanced up at him. "You don't believe what he said?"

"I do, but I still want to keep an eye on him until we learn more."

Women rushed between rooms, half-dressed, scarves flying, tops and bottoms being yanked on. Breasts bouncing, a woman ran by, bumping into Markus. The performer grabbed his arm, looking like she was using him as balance.

"Oh, oops," she giggled and planted Markus's hand right on her breast.

Bella clenched her teeth and reached to swat the woman's hands off her husband. But a throat cleared.

"Well, if you don't know what to do with such a lovely handful, I can instruct you," a harsh, gravelly voice said. "After all, you don't have so much woman in your bed. Tell me, do you miss breasts, beast master?"

Twice now, a man had commented on Bella's lack of feminine curves. Her fingers curled into her palm. She ignored Hossman's crude words and glared at the woman. "Let go of my husband."

Markus snatched his hand free and wiped his palm on his pants. "Do you force men to touch you often?"

The woman flushed and sniffed. "I was giving you a free taste, that's all honey. No need to get mad."

"I'll take a taste," Hossman said, sliding closer. He touched a finger to the woman's arm. "What room are you in?"

The performer shrugged away his caress. "Five. Starts in two."

Hossman licked his thin lips. "I'll be watching. Make it good for me."

"I always make it good," the woman said, lifting her pointed chin. She rushed off, her pale butt cheeks bouncing and gleaming in the candlelit corridor.

Hossman swiped a hand down his mouth. "Look at that, would you? Not something I could turn down. Mm-mmm." His attention shifted to Bella. "Never thought I'd see you in a place like this. Need some excitement in your marriage already? Not that I'm surprised. I can't imagine a Sziverian can meet the demands of a Ruthenian." He tsked. "Should have asked her to give you some advice instead of snarling."

The horrid man didn't give either of them a chance to speak, hurrying after the disappearing performer, tripping in his haste. He swiped a hand to right himself on the wall, barely missing a lantern. Bella's gaze narrowed.

"It's him, I know it," she whispered.

Markus shook his head and pulled her along to the lobby. "It's not him."

Clenching her hands, Bella fell in step beside him. "Intimidating the competition before he makes a bid would be just what Hossman would do."

"I doubt Burnsean asked for Hossman's help five months ago."

"So maybe Hossman is working with other owners. He's a crime boss."

Markus stopped at the front desk and knocked his knuckles on the wood. A woman wearing a scrap of fabric over her full, unsupported breasts and a sheer flowing red skirt suspended from a chain around her belly sauntered from behind a curtain. She wiped her mouth, a naughty light in her eyes.

"May I help you?" she asked. A man hurried from behind the curtain, both hands clutching the waist of his unbuttoned pants, a jacket dangling from his forearm. She glanced at him and giggled. "Enjoy the show, James." Once the man disappeared, she returned her attention to Markus. "Do you need a little pre-show encouragement, too?"

Bella grabbed Markus's elbow. The proposition was the last straw. "Forget about the free show. We won't be returning."

"Bella..."

"No," she ground out and glared at the hussy behind the counter. "We're leaving."

The woman propped her chin on her hand and kissed the air. "I don't blame you, honey. I'd keep all that to myself, too. Lucky."

Bella had to get out of the building before *she* set a fire. She released Markus and rushed past a group of laughing men near the door to the cool night beyond. A touch ghosted across her shoulders, and she shied away.

"Don't," she bit out. She knew the anger bouncing around inside her was misplaced. Being the more attractive half of their pairing wasn't Markus's fault. He hadn't asked or invited any of the attention shown toward him. "I just need a minute."

"Do you want to go home?" he asked quietly, moving to stand near the curb.

Bella lifted her chin. "No, I want to go to Velvet and Candlelight. Find out if the owner there did business with Hossman."

Markus's jaw tightened. "I already told you it's not him."

"Why? We don't know for certain when they started doing business. We didn't check to see when Burnsean lost the bid on the hotel." Bella waved a hand at the building four stories higher than the curtain show house nestled on the corner. "Maybe Hossman is getting into a new aspect of his criminal antics. Maybe he wants to make sure his five percent is padded. Less competition, more people will be going to Burnsean's new establishment, which will include *both* the businesses where fires have started."

Markus leaned forward, his nose nearly touching hers, the gold of his eyes blazing. "It's not him. You're allowing your past with him to color your view."

Maybe. Hossman's reputation didn't leave much room for doubt in her mind, however. "He's a weasel."

"*Dak*, I do not disagree, but he's not burning curtain show houses."

Bella's nostrils flared as his scent drifted on the subtle breeze around her. The forest after rain. The bite of leather. Markus. Bella wanted to close the very short distance between them and press her nose into the cords of his neck. Lick. Bite. Do all the things she wasn't allowed to. Instead, she took a careful step back and reminded herself she was furious, not to mention a bit humiliated. Being rebuffed by him again would lead to a meltdown she had too much dignity to permit.

"You can't know he isn't involved for certain," she said.

He straightened and pointed at the show house. "His dick was so hard it was sticking out the top of his pants. The only thought he had was how to either convince a woman to handle it for him or handle it himself in the privacy of a showroom. I guarantee you, anytime he sets foot into a show house, a competitor of this establishment or not, his thoughts are not on how to destroy the place but where he can go to come the fastest. Hossman is not our culprit."

Some of her ire faded. The visuals of his words made her grimace. "Ew."

"I agree. I can't unsee *anything* I saw in there." He shook his head and fisted his hands on his hips, facing the street. "I hate this. Had I known about the subculture, I wouldn't have taken the case."

"There aren't curtain show houses in Ruthenia?"

He pointed a thumb over his shoulder. "Not like this. The few we have are limited to the port cities, where travelers can partake, and singles know where to go for fun. A mate wouldn't tolerate their partner going to one, so they don't do well in the inner cities. Plus, they can only be open three or four months a year, so it doesn't make sense to put them some-where they won't be profitable."

Bella looked at the painted window with the business name. "I don't think any of the houses are quite like this. Burnsean seems to like the lewd and shocking."

"Perhaps." He ran both hands down his face. "You still want to go to Velvet and Candle-light tonight?"

"It'll be near midnight. Clientele will be at its peak, so maybe, like here, the owner will be around, and we can learn more about the fire."

"If anyone says anything to you there..." He shook his head. "Maybe we should do this to-morrow night."

"Tonight, tomorrow, I'll be just as upset about you being propositioned. At least we know what to expect now," she argued. "I want to finish the case. Putting off a visit will just delay possibly learning something by another day."

Markus wanted to argue waiting another day would allow them time to decompress. Give him the opportunity to try to undo the damage done by those who looked at his wife and saw a woman lacking. But the only way Markus knew to convince her of her beauty, of how desirable she was to him, could only be done by his hands and mouth on her skin. An internal battle he was precariously close to losing.

He still hadn't decided if he'd return and punch Burnsean in the face when the case closed, and he no longer needed the man's co-operation. He truly might. Hossman and Lunah would cross paths again at some point. The infuriating crime boss popped into Markus's sphere at unexpected moments. He regretted leaving his wolf home. Hossman wouldn't have dared speak to Bella, let alone insult her, had Lunah been present.

Hailing down a cabby, Markus took Bella's hand and pulled her to the curb with him. A coach stopped, and Markus gave the destination and helped Bella inside. The interior stunk of unwashed bodies and other things he didn't want to consider. Hailing a street carriage was always a risk. When possible, he preferred a higher-end service. But it was midnight, and their local offered no other options.

Bella hesitated to sit on the narrow, rough wood plank seat. Markus closed them in, making sure the curtains were open to allow the maximum amount of fresh air. The evening was mild enough that they wouldn't get too cold. He sat and pulled her onto his thighs.

She squeaked in shock and stiffened. "Is this wise?"

"Probably not," he admitted, wrapping his arms around her narrow waist. He rested his chin on her shoulder. "But I don't want you sitting on the filth."

And he missed her. So much.

The carriage jolted over each uneven brick on the road. Markus tightened his hold to keep her from bouncing free. The heat of her skin through the cotton blend of her tunic teased his fingertips. He wanted to lift her shirt and the smooth flesh of her hips and stomach. Trace the lines of his imprint on her back.

Slowing, the carriage rocked to a stop at their location. A woman's forced laughter joined a glass bottle dropping and men whooping in drunken merriment. Markus helped Bella, keeping her in sight as he leaped from the interior to the sidewalk. He paid their fare and surveyed their surroundings.

Two men had their arms draped over the shoulders of a curvy woman. She shimmied and guided them to the brightly lit doorway of

Velvet and Candlelight. The man on the left opened the door. With another bark of amusement, she urged them inside, swatting one on the butt, her words lost against their laughter. The second the door swung shut behind them, her shoulders sagged, and her spine bowed. She rubbed her temples, her foot catching the bottle one of the men had dropped. The brown glass spun and bounced off the curb into the street, causing the horse to knicker in annoyance. Realizing she wasn't alone any longer, the performer slid back into her role, a smile curving her lips that didn't reach her eyes.

"We're not customers. You can relax," Bella said. Markus was unsurprised she'd noticed the woman's fatigue.

"Everyone's a customer, beauty," the woman purred, her hips swinging in a slow glide as she neared them. "I promise you'll change your mind the moment you set foot inside. Let me show you what the night can bring."

"We're investigating the fire that happened here a few months ago," Bella said. "Were you working that night?"

The woman shrugged, adjusting the scrap of red lace over her breasts that draped to her hips. "It was an accident. Someone knocked a lamp over. Mitch, a guy the owner allows to work those rooms, caught it before the fire could destroy much. They've already fixed it, so don't worry, all the rooms are available." She eased toward the door. "Come on, I'll personally show you around. You can decide if you want to stay."

"Can we talk to Mitch?" Bella asked.

"Yeah, I think I saw him tonight," she said, pushing open the door. Her gaze wandered over Bella, and Markus resisted the urge to step in front of his mate. "I can't promise he'll be able to speak with you, however. Time with you will be time he won't have with a customer. Of course, he may agree to give you information easier if you're a customer. Let me show you to a room."

Bella stiffened. "We're—"

"That's fine," Markus said, taking her hand and squeezing. "Show us to one of Mitch's rooms. We'll work a deal out that's satisfactory for both of us."

"Follow me." Sashaying her full hips, the lace of her black skirt trailing along the carpeted floor a rich shade of emerald, she led them to a desk. "Sign in here."

Bella accepted a pen from a young blonde woman behind the counter. The receptionist pointed to a line, and Bella scrawled her name. "Do you have the logs from the night of the fire?"

"Fire?" the blonde asked, blinking her gray-green eyes.

The performer waved her hand. "I'll handle it, Em. You didn't work here yet."

"Ah. Thanks, Krissa. I've already been in trouble tonight for not remembering a rule. I don't think Ginger would be happy if I did it again." Em accepted the pen from Bella.

Krissa patted the blonde's arm. "Ginger can be tough, but you'll learn." She turned and faced Bella. "I'll bring the log book to you. Let's continue. I know just the room. Plenty big enough for three."

"We won't be staying for an entire show," Bella said, her steps hurrying to catch Krissa. "Can you bring the logs to us as soon as possible?"

Krissa's smile was brittle as she stopped next to a curtained entryway. "I'll give the book to Mitch, how's that?"

"Great," Bella bit out, her frustration sliding across their bond.

"Enjoy," Krissa sang, jerking the thick velvet curtain shut.

Bella blew out a long sigh and looked around the closet-sized room. Two chairs were arranged in front of a glass wall, a closed curtain on the outside. Markus grasped the back of the chair nearest to him and took in the rest of the room. Nude paintings of men and women in provocative poses or pleasuring themselves framed the wall from the chair rail to the ceiling. A single candle flickered from a suspended glass bowl above them. Enough light to not be encased in darkness, but not enough to cause any kind of reflection that would impede the view through the glass.

"Charming," Bella muttered. "I wonder how long until—"

The curtain swooshed open, and a shirtless man in loose silk pants carrying a leather case and a thick bound book grinned at them. His black hair fell in disheveled waves to his shoulders in the back and feathered around his face. A fine sheen of sweat gleamed on his skin. He was smaller than Markus, less muscled, and a little soft around the hips, but that didn't stop Markus from wanting to punch his teeth out.

"I'm Mitch. Krissa said you requested me?" He quickly offered the book to Markus. "And I'm to give you this?"

Markus accepted the log. The man squeezed the rest of the way into the room. Bella relocated to the corner behind Markus, her hands fisting in the back of his shirt.

"You are Mitch?" Markus asked.

"I am," the man answered, inclining his head. He set the bundle of leather on a chair. "So, what's it to be? A little voyeurism while you watch the show? A little mutual pleasure with assistance?"

"A little talking," Markus said.

Mitch glanced at Markus, then to Bella, and back to Markus. "Talking?" Comprehension dawned on his face, and he laughed. "Ah yes, I understand. I will give you a conversation you won't soon forget. What's your fantasy? Imagined threesome?"

Markus pinched the bridge of his nose. Would every person they encountered in these curtain show houses think only of sex? He supposed since people came for one thing, one thing was all they expected. "No fantasy. No sexual favors. We need to ask you a few questions about the fire. We were told you were the one to put it out."

Skepticism pinched Mitch's face and narrowed his gaze. "What is this?"

"We will pay you whatever your rate is for your time, but you will keep all parts of your body to yourself," Markus clarified.

Mitch picked up the bundle, holding it to his side. "I charge more for pairs."

"Understandable. What is your price?"

Mitch licked his lips, his gaze flickering to the glass wall as he named his price. "And the curtain has to be open, or Ginger will become suspicious. I'm only allowed to work rooms of paying curtain show customers."

"Work rooms?" Bella asked, leaning around Markus. "Like give a private show?"

Mitch glanced between them again. "I'm a sex hustler. I thought Krissa told you."

Markus had guessed as much. Bella's squeak of alarm meant his more innocent wife had not.

Mitch clenched his jaw. "I'm safe. I'm clean. HRS is bad for business, and since the location of the incident is listed, if an HRS outbreak happens here, customers will stay away for at least two weeks. Ginger has a rule. No penetration sex. None of the workers she allows inside break the rule. If caught, they're banned. I need this job. I have two daughters at home. I can't afford to bring home a deadly virus any more than Ginger can afford to have one occur in her show house."

Slowly, Mitch unrolled the leather satchel. Glass phalluses in various shapes, sizes, and adornments shimmered in the low light. One had shallow green spirals all the way around. Another had dark blue bumps. One had a head shaped like a pink rose, complete with green leaves. Another had two small prongs near the base. One was barely the size of his pinky, while another made him raise a brow. It was thicker than his wrist.

"They're fully sanitized," Mitch said, fingering a glass member with a faint tapered curve at the end. "I can demonstrate my skills if you'd like."

Markus leaned forward, his gaze locked with the hustlers. "You come near my wife with any of those, and I will help you find a new place to shove it. Do you understand?"

The hustler visibly swallowed. The case curled closed. "I was just—"

"There is no *just* anything," Markus growled. "We did not ask for you to do anything other than give us information, which I offered to pay your rate for. Do you understand?"

"Y-yes," Mitch whispered, color bleaching from his face. "I'm sorry."

Markus straightened. "*Dhorsh.*" Good.

Mitch pointed at the glass wall. "We still need to, ah, open this, though."

Bella stepped to Markus's side. She dug

around inside her satchel and removed a wallet. She pulled free a handful of raimarks. "I'm not sure..."

Mitch's hand reached for the bills and hovered. "May I?"

Bella nodded. Mitch plucked a few bills free and turned, feeding them into a slot.

"Take what else you need," Markus said, motioning at the money.

While the curtain inched upward, Mitch pulled his fee from Bella's fingers. Bright light spilled into the room from the glass wall. A completely naked, fully erect man undulated his lower body in a mimic of slow sex on a circular stage. Oil coated his skin, drawing attention to each shift and flex of his muscled form. He smoothed a hand down his hairless chest to palm his erection.

"Oh, stars above," Bella breathed and spun, putting her back to the glass, her hands covering her eyes. The remaining raimarks fluttered to the floor.

The performer dropped to his knees and kept one hand on himself while the other braced on the floor. He curved his spine to lift his butt before swooping his hips low as if entering a lover, obviously fulfilling multiple fantasies with one routine.

"The fire," Markus prompted, easily looking away as the act became cruder.

Mitch tore his gaze from the performance. "I was working with a client when I smelled smoke. No one had noticed yet. The room nearest to the fire was vacant. I'm not sure if anyone had been in the room and had left or if someone was in a hurry to get to a room and knocked a lantern over, but that's all that happened."

"A lantern had been knocked over?"

Mitch shook his head. "No, not just knocked over, swept completely off the table. The glass had broken, and the burning wick had caught the curtain to a viewing room on fire. I pulled the curtain down and grabbed another from the next room to douse the flames."

"Is it done yet?" Bella asked.

"Even if it were, the curtain would have to be kept open for the next show if you wish to talk," Mitch said. "But I don't know what else to tell you."

"Did you know any of the patrons in the nearby rooms?" Markus asked.

"No, none of them were regulars."

Markus balanced the book on his left arm and opened the cover. Not only were names and dates listed, but so were the rooms the visitors had been placed in. "Which room was the fire started at?"

Mitch leaned close. Sweat and sex drifted from his skin, and Markus scrunched his nose.

"Um, let me see. Ah, here. The room was C five." Mitch touched the paper. "The room across from it is A seven. But if it was just someone passing through, you'll never learn that."

Markus handed the book to Bella. "Can you

copy the night of the fire and two weeks prior?" Then he met Mitch's gaze. "Is there another show immediately when this one is finished?"

"Yes. Ginger doesn't have any intermissions. Anyone can walk in anytime and open a curtain for a show in any viewing room." Mitch leaned down and picked up the fallen bills. "You'll need these if you wish to stay. I can get you an evening entertainment guide if you'd like so you know what the next performance will include."

"Thank you, but we won't be watching, so it doesn't matter."

Mitch nodded. "Right. Well, if that's all?"

"*Dak,* thank you."

The sex hustler left, the velvet curtain swaying closed behind him. Markus grabbed the chairs and flipped them around, placing their backs to the vulgar finale happening on the mini stage.

"Maybe the fire that happened here really was an accident," Bella muttered, opening the book on her lap. She dug around inside her bag and removed her notebook and a pencil. "Everyone else has been suspicious, but here they were adamant someone knocked over a lantern by bumping into a table."

"Let's see what the sign-in logs show. We'll check the others that weren't destroyed at the rest of the affected businesses. Maybe we'll get lucky, and the person didn't think about using a fake name."

Tension stiffened her shoulders and made

her motions jerky. Markus tilted his head back and looked at the decorative tiles lining the ceiling. He wanted to touch her. Desperately. Instead, he stared at the hard shadows gathered along the sculpted edges and flowery designs of the tiles. Moments later, the quiet whir of the curtain closing made him twist in his seat.

"Do you have much longer?" he asked.

"A little bit. I want to record this entire hall, just in case."

Markus searched and found the slot for the money. He followed the directions, and after a few seconds, the curtain slid upward. Candles safe under glass globes surrounded the circular stage with no other light. A female form undulated under sheer sage green silk sheets. The fabric slid away in small increments with each twist of her abdomen, lift of her leg or arm, or rise of her full breasts, revealing golden brown skin. A section glided from her breast to land on the floor. Her fingers sought out her dark brown nipple, pinching and pulling in the same motion as her hips. Markus couldn't help but imagine Bella in such a provocative manner on their bed, the sheets covering everything he wanted to see while she teased him with her fingers on her body.

Quickly, he spun away from the view, his nails digging into his thighs. Bella's head snapped up. She looked at him, over her shoulder, and back to him. Anger and hurt ignited across their bond, searing a path straight to his heart. She rotated in the chair and watched, her jaw clenching. Jealousy added to the already intense emotional onslaught.

"You're missing something you clearly enjoyed. Don't stop watching on my account," she ground out, rising. The book snapped closed, and she fought with the flap of her messenger bag to get her journal and pencil back inside. Anything he said would make things worse, so he kept his mouth shut and reached to help, but she snatched her hands away and stepped out of his range. "I have it."

The curtain swooshed open, and a buxom redhead wearing a pink dress that only covered one side of her body propped her arm above her head on the frame and slid her fingers along the edge of the draping skirt between her legs. "Hello, in the mood for a little—"

"Move," Bella snapped, shoving past the woman when she didn't vacate the entry in a timely manner.

Markus hopped up.

The woman stumbled backward. "Hey! You could have just said no!"

Markus rushed after his fleeing wife. "Bella, wait!"

No matter what he said, he wouldn't be able to convince her anything she felt from him wasn't a result of the performance. Markus didn't know how to fix this. He ran after her, wondering if a similar scene had led to the fire so many months ago. He certainly had to maneuver with quick reflexes to avoid running into other patrons and the sex hustlers hurrying between rooms. These houses of debauchery were grating on his every nerve when he had none left to spare.

Bella disappeared around a corner, where they'd entered the building. Skidding across the carpet, he caught the jam to stop his momentum and yanked himself into the lobby. The woman behind the desk squeaked as Bella tossed the log book on the counter without stopping. The digest landed with a heavy thud, sliding across the counter and over the edge. The bell over the door gave a hard jangle as Bella sent the wood swinging on its hinges.

Three snickering men hunched over a pamphlet stumbled into Markus's path on their way to find a show. Markus spun around them and beelined for the closing door. The hard fall of Bella's shoes echoed on the sidewalk. The hostess, Krissa, was thankfully nowhere to be seen. Markus didn't need an audience to his mistake.

Fix her, Alpha, fix her! Lunah beseeched in his mind, the discord between him and his mate trickling to his wolf. *Happy, make my Bella happy!*

Markus sighed and increased his pace, catching Bella's elbow and spinning them into the privacy of a narrow alley. He dragged her deeper into the shadowy depths, listening to ensure they were indeed alone. When no rustling clothing, ragged breaths, or moans broke the silence, he pushed her against a brick wall and caged her in.

"Let me go," she snapped. "I want to go home."

"Then we'll go home, but first, we're going to talk, you and I."

"There is nothing to discuss." She shoved at his chest. "I am not eno—"

His mouth captured hers, stealing away the lie she would have spoken. He swept his tongue past her lips, catching her teeth, tasting her fire. She switched from shoving him away to dragging him closer. His torso collided with hers, sending her slamming into the brick wall. The hard jolt didn't faze either of them. Cool air brushed his skin seconds before her fingers dug into his flanks beneath his shirt. Arcs of lightning danced across her touch, along with her desire. His entire focus narrowed down to her. What she wanted. What she *needed*.

Hard and throbbing, his only goal was to remove enough clothes to have her. All other rational thought fled. Her tongue tangled with his. Her nails scored his sides and his back in her desperation. Markus broke the kiss long enough to fumble with the buttons of his pants.

"Summer sun, yes, *yes*," she moaned, popping off a shoe and one pant leg. The second her foot was free, she grappled with his shoulders, trying to climb his body.

Markus didn't waste a second helping her. His hands slid under her butt, shoving fabric out of the way. He hoisted her up against the wall, splitting her thighs around his waist.

"Hurry, hurry," she gasped, her hips arching to find him.

Adjusting her weight to one arm, Markus reached between them to grab his erection. Resisting the urge to stroke himself, he tested her entrance with the tip, easily sliding along her slick folds. Groaning, he pressed inside, easing into her silken heat an inch at a time until he was deep enough to return his hand to support her. Little mewling sounds escaped her mouth. She worked her hips, taking him deeper, the snug hold of her inner muscles shattering his control.

Markus somehow managed to position her so he could lift her tunic to bring her breast to his mouth. He wanted to feel her shatter around him. Wanted to experience the fist of her orgasm and rock her into another. He wanted her pleasure barreling through him, enhancing his own. *Zhak'tu,* he just *wanted.* And he'd learned over the past couple of months that if he took her nipple into his mouth, sucked the hard nub, bit a little, sucked a lot harder, she'd—

One of her hands yanked on his braid while the other gripped his shoulder hard enough to press her nails through his shirt and into his skin. Her back arched, and every muscle tightened as an incoherent sound growled deep in her throat. Her release coated his length, making each thrust easier until he pounded into her without fear of hurting her.

Markus shifted her again, hooking both her legs over his forearms, pushing her thighs further apart, allowing him to plunge deeper. She cried out, her head lolling. The column of her throat beckoned, and he latched on, sucking, licking, biting until she was once again wild, hurtling toward another climax.

Still wasn't enough for him. He pulled back. Met her glazed stare. "Touch yourself for me," he growled.

"Markus," she whimpered, twisting, desperate for more.

"Do it, *krahet'snu*."

She slid her hand between them and worked her clit, her hips jolting in time with each forceful roll of his. She knew what he wanted and didn't make him ask for it, bringing her fingers coated in her desire to his mouth. He sucked them in, tasting her passion. She erupted, coming so hard she squeezed her eyes closed and clenched her teeth. Exactly what he'd needed. The tight spasms of her orgasm pulled him deep into her, milking his hot seed free. Markus's body jerked, and he grunted, each intense jet of his release flowing in a wave of intense pleasure. She yanked her fingers from his mouth, continuing to come, her breathing harsh and shallow, her back arching, her hips rocking to prologue the gratification. Markus rolled his hips, the sensation of her climax too good to stop, even as he emptied into her.

Slowly, they stilled, their breathing ragged gasps of vapor in the cold of early morning. Markus licked his lips and rested his forehead on the chilled bricks beside her head. Her luscious scent wrapped further around him, reminding him he'd be ready for her again. Soon.

"Are you all right?" he whispered.

She kissed his cheek above his beard and chuckled weakly. "If I were any better, I'd float away." When he remained quiet, she whispered, "Are you okay?"

Markus couldn't quantify how he felt. Sated. Relieved their bond no longer had a tension. Content. And yet, he knew, without any doubt, they'd just created life.

CHAPTER

EIGHT

THE PINK GLOW OF SUNRISE BLOOMED ACROSS THE ceiling and cast long shadows along the walls and floor. Bella trailed her hand through Markus's unbound hair, allowing the silky length to glide through her fingers until she encountered his skin, and then she'd start over. After hours of hard sex, even dirtier than their round in the alley, he'd finally collapsed on his stomach, still half on her, too exhausted to take her again. He'd fallen asleep with a hand on her breast, his thigh wedged between hers, and his face turned away.

Bella had no such luck. She ached in delicious ways and was sticky from sweat and her husband's spent desire. The sheets would need changing when they finally began their day. And still, she wanted him. Tingled and throbbed to feel him hard for her and her alone. A selfish, guilt-riddled reaction that kept her awake.

She'd known her outburst at Velvet and

Candlelight had been immature and un-founded, yet she'd been too on edge to prevent the response. Her only regret was Markus being emotionally blackmailed into giving in to the lust neither had been able to deny. She'd felt his desperation to fix what he perceived as unfixable. Had been incapable of telling him to stop when he'd undone his pants. And she hated herself a little for the way everything had happened.

The rough, almost punishing way he'd taken her from the moment they walked into their bedroom made her wonder if he were angry at her, too. She'd tried to sift through the emotions filtering along their bond, but only desire had blazed an unmistakable trail. She wanted to be relieved but couldn't shake the uneasiness of her mistake.

Laying in the calm of morning, she tried to convince herself she wasn't pregnant. Markus wouldn't miss out on one of the most impor-tant moments of their lives. Near the end of her fertile time, there was a slight chance nothing would come of their giving into temptation. She fisted the strands of his hair and breathed his scent in deep, squeezing her eyes closed. When she found out for sure, she'd be alone. She couldn't change that reality.

Maybe he'd have access to a radio, and she could radio him the day she found out. When the weeks on the calendar confirmed her missed monthly. Bella clung to the thought as she finally drifted to sleep.

She awoke when the sun fully brightened the room to her husband between her spread thighs, easing her into passion with gentle caresses of his fingers. When she managed to make her voice work enough to beg, he climbed her body. He carefully pressed into her, loving her in slow, measured thrusts, working her into a quiet yet intense release. He continued rocking his hips, kissing her jaw, throat, and collarbone. Love blazed between their bond, hurtling her into another climax he joined her in, the heat of his release filling her.

Afterward, he held her while she trembled. "Good morning, *krahet'sna*."

Many mornings had started this way, and Bella almost cried at how much she missed the gentle intimacy, even though only three mornings had technically passed since she'd been without. The stress of refraining made it seem like three years. She tilted her head to look out the window. "Is it still morning?"

He shifted, causing him to move within her, buried as he still was, and she moaned. "I'm not sure. I think my shirt is covering the clock, and I can't reach it."

Bella twisted and saw, yes, his shirt had landed on the clock in the chaos of their arousal when they'd arrived home. She giggled.

Groaning, Markus pulled free and rolled off the bed. He held out his hand. "Come on, let's shower and eat, and I want to map the fires. I had a thought."

She set her hand in his, her belly flipping at his raw sexuality and male beauty. His member hung thick between his thighs, dark and glistening from their lovemaking. The cords of his muscles were on full display in the harsh afternoon sun streaming through the windows. Every inch of his cinnamon-caramel skin beckoned her. He hauled her up and guided her to the spacious shower stall in their bathroom.

The luxury of hot water soon pounded on slate tiles. Markus entered first and pulled her inside with him. She leaned against the cold stone wall and enjoyed following the rivulets of water chasing each other down his torso to his thighs. The shower seemed to be the only place he was comfortable allowing her to explore him, though he often limited her to a few tantalizing caresses before he took her in creative ways. As a result, her imagination always wandered, taking their play to new heights, which always led to actual play, even if it wasn't what she ultimately desired.

This morning was different. While she appreciated it, her mind didn't move beyond. "Are you upset?" she asked, barely audible over the pound of water.

"No," he answered, tilting back his head to wet his hair.

Bella wasn't sure she believed him. She pressed her hands behind her back, her bare butt against her knuckles. "Why?"

Hair wet and slicked back, he reached for the shampoo. "We were both in that alley."

"But I—"

He leaned forward and pressed a quick kiss to her lips. "No," he whispered and then returned to washing his hair. "You did nothing wrong. Those curtain houses..." He shook his head, white foam sliding to his shoulder. "They are depraved and pushed us to our breaking point. What happened, happened."

Bella wanted to believe him, but guilt gnawed at her mind. "I know, but—"

He kissed her again. "You have nothing to feel ashamed of. I'm the one who couldn't wait. I'm the one who took you like a sex hustler in an alley. I'm—"

Bella hopped onto her toes and wrapped her arms around his neck. "You wanted me," she said, tears burning her eyes at the memory of his desperation. At knowing she, *Bella*, was his sole focus, all he wanted. The level of his need hadn't reached such heights for anyone else.

Hugging her tight, he pressed his face into her throat. "I will always want you. Always. *Dsi tul'me*. Only you. Never doubt again."

They stood locked in a tight hug until Markus pulled her under, water spraying in her face. She laughed and shoved him away, wetting her hair. He tossed her the soap bottle while reaching for a bar to finish washing. Their easy dance of switching places to wash or rinse made Bella smile. Another morning ritual she'd missed in the short time she'd been denied. Somehow, she resisted the urge to slide her hands along his slickened skin and feel his arousal grow, both physically and through their bond. An experience she didn't think she'd ever find tiring.

Finished, he stepped from the shower. "I will get us some food if you find a map of Haven City."

"Get us some food as in...?" Bella asked, rinsing the conditioner from her curls.

"Lunah needs to walk. What are you in the mood for?"

Bella considered all the options he'd pass depending on his route. Since moving to the complex, she'd discovered all sorts of delicious bakeries and specialty food vendors. "Oh, how about those fruit pastries from Anna's Pies and the fried meat, no wait, the sweet and spicy bacon from Sweets and Savorys? And some spiced apples from that fruit stand near the square?"

He laughed and tossed a fluffy ivory towel over the glass door. "Hungry?"

"Famished," she admitted, turning off the water. She pulled down the towel and pressed the soft fabric to her face. "Your fault."

"I'm going to feed you. Promise." Cool air rushed into the stall, and she was being hauled into strong arms. He peeled the towel from her face and kissed her. "I love you."

Her arms were trapped between them, hugging the towel. Warmth blossomed in her chest and spread to her feet. She rose on her toes and returned his kiss. "I love you, too. Now, walk our girl and get us some food."

He growled and took her mouth in a searing kiss, then broke away just as fast, leaving chilled air between them. Bella stumbled and reached out for the counter.

Towel pressed to his groin, Markus shook his head. "I'm sorry. No more, not until tonight."

Bella waved, clutching the towel to her chest. "Go. Close the door."

He gave her one last heated glance before putting a door between them. She knew if she were to push him, to saunter in there and toss her towel aside, lay on the bed, spread her legs, and—

"Bella! Stop!" His words muffled through the door.

She laughed, wanting to tease him more, yet knowing her ovulation phase, though thankfully near the end, still had him on edge. Too much temptation and her sore body would be enduring another pleasurable round. She had to agree she needed a break, or she wouldn't be walking anywhere today. At the solid thud of the door to their bedroom closing, Bella ventured from the bathroom, drying her hair. Their closet door had been left open, as had the entrance to the sunroom. A sweet outdoor breeze floated into the room, diffusing some of Bella's annoyance. She leaned into the closet and grabbed a loose, navy, peach-striped knit shirt and a calf-length flowing silk cream skirt. A pair of brown leather boots would round out her outfit.

Dressed, hair pulled into a twist atop her head, she went to the radio room and dug around for a city map. After setting the rolled paper on the living room table, she returned to the bedroom and cleaned up the mess they'd made the night before. Sheets changed. Clothing tossed in the hamper. She checked on Lunah's space, giving the wolf new water and fixing her pillow bed, which she'd decided to wrestle with at some point.

An explosion of feathers on the other side of the screened room had Bella searching for a hole in the mesh that a bird had managed to squeeze inside to its doom. Squinting, she spotted an area at the top where the screen appeared to have come undone from the edge. She tugged a chair from the small sitting area near the door to the damaged panel. Positioning the seat, she climbed up, balancing on the frame. On her tiptoes, she picked at the opening. She never would have guessed anything, much less a bird with enough feathers to look like a burst pillow, could have fit through. She tried to roll the mesh back into place but couldn't see where the thin borders came together to tuck it back. Biting her bottom lip, she balanced on the chair arms to give her a few more inches.

Focused on the task, she failed to realize she wasn't alone. "What are you doing?"

A scream erupted from her throat, and she

lost her balance. Memories of tumbling down an endless hole, not knowing what awaited her, stole across her vision. Strong arms snatched her from the air. Bella flailed until the scent of Markus invaded her senses. His hold on her tightened, hugging her to his chest.

"You're okay," he whispered against her temple. "Shh, you're safe."

She breathed in ragged bursts, her heart thundering in her ears. She licked her dry lips and clutched at his shirt. "I was trying... a bird... Lunah."

Markus carried her into their bedroom and sat on the edge of the mattress. He settled her on his lap and rubbed his palm between her shoulder blades. "Slow down and just breathe. In, out, in."

He repeated the mantra. Bella listened and obeyed, breathing as he instructed. The panic attacks had been an unexpected development after their return from Thanzia. Waking up in the dark had sent her back to the underground caves, the stench of death heavy in the air. Without Markus, she didn't know what she would have done. Probably crawled into bed with her mother. The fear subsided with each measured inhale and gentle exhale.

"I'm okay," she whispered, straightening, releasing her grip on his clothes. "I'm all right now."

He kissed the top of her head and then helped her stand.

Bella motioned toward the open door outside. "There's a hole in the screen. Lunah ate a bird. I was trying to fix it."

He tucked a fallen curl behind her ear. "I'll take care of it. Food is in the living room."

Arguing would be useless, so she nodded and went to find what he'd brought home. Lunah sat in front of the low table, licking her chops, her gaze fixed on a paper bag with grease spots. Bella raised her brows and laughed.

"Are you starving?" she asked. Lunah's ears perked, and she twisted her head around, golden eyes bright.

Bella, my Bella!

Lunah bounded over the couch, yipping. Bella leaned over and captured the wolf's soft neck, hugging her tight. "Hey, sweet girl. I saw you caught a poor bird."

Feathers stuck to my tongue, feathers stuck. A sneeze punctuated the statement.

Bella ruffled the fur between Lunah's shoulder blades and stood. "I have no sympathy for you."

Lunah danced back to the table, spinning and hopping in place.

Bella picked up the bag and carried it to the kitchen. She pulled down three plates, placing them in a row. "Let's see what we have."

A delicious feast of fruit stuffed pastries, sticky, sweet, spiced bacon, and two jars of cinnamon apples. Meat pies were at the bottom for Lunah. Bella divided everything between the three plates.

"There's another bag behind you with butcher scraps," Markus said as he walked into the living room.

Bella twisted and noted the twine-wrapped wax package. Inside were chunks of fat, gristle, and chopped organ meat. She dumped the contents on top of the meat pies and handed the plate across to Markus, along with his dish. He took both to the dining table and did the eating routine with an eager Lunah. After washing her hands, Bella carried her food to the living room, curious to learn why Markus needed the map. The snuffling and chomp of Lunah eating soon filled the living space.

Markus joined her on the couch, setting his plate beside hers. "Do you want to take a break from investigating tonight?"

Embarrassment flushed Bella's cheeks. She hated the moment of insecurity that made him question her ability to continue the investigation. Folding a gooey slice of bacon into her mouth, she shook her head. "No. We need to solve this before you have to leave."

His fingers brushed her wrist, drawing her attention to him. Warmth filled his gaze. "I didn't ask because I felt you incapable. I asked because..." He gently swept a curl behind her ear, his touch drifting to caress her jaw. "I was not gentle with you this morning, and neither of us are functioning on much sleep."

The hours of wild sex flared through her mind. No, until they woke up, he'd been everything except *gentle*. Out of control, passionate, dominating... and she'd loved every rough minute. So much so she had to press her thighs together and bury the sudden ache of need. She took another bite, stuffing her mouth for distraction.

"I'm okay," she muffled out, covering her mouth.

He smiled and reached for his food. Before eating, he took a deep breath. "Your scent is fading back to normal. We should be about free of my crazy reaction."

She swallowed and reached for a napkin. "I like your crazy."

He shifted on the couch, bracing his hand on his knee. "Yeah?"

Licking the sticky from her fingers, she nodded. "I figured my demands for more while screaming made it clear how much I enjoyed, you know, us."

"Mmm." He leaned close and kissed her, his tongue licking a path into her mouth. "I still can't believe there is an us," he whispered against her lips, "I keep expecting to wake up, and I do, but you're beside me."

"I feel the same," she admitted, caressing his bearded jaw. "Do you think we'll ever stop feeling in awe of being together?"

"*Dak*, but that doesn't mean we have to stop appreciating our relationship."

He kissed her again. Longer. Deeper. Until she wanted to climb on his lap and make good use of having worn a skirt.

Pulling back before they could lose all focus, she touched a finger to his damp bottom lip. "We almost made it. Are you upset? Honestly?"

He grasped her hand and kissed her palm. "*Vye*, I'm not. No point, is there? I meant what I said earlier. We were both present. Neither of us forced the other in that alley."

Bella wanted to push the subject, but he pressed another quick kiss to her lips and returned to his food. One hand held a pastry while the other sent the map unrolling across the table.

"All right," he huffed, brushing crumbs from his fingers. "Can you read off the addresses to all the fires?"

Bella tried to remember where her messenger bag had landed in their chaotic haste to make it to the bedroom. She hadn't picked it up with everything else.... Tapping her fingers on her knees, she glanced around the living room. Her shoes were off to the left of the door, one upside down, the other a few feet away. The bag lay half open in front of the wood stove. A pen and the pamphlet from one of the curtain show houses spilled out. She rose and grabbed the bag, pulling out her notebook before tossing the rest onto the end of the couch. While she'd retrieved her things, Markus had disappeared into the small radio room. He returned carrying a wooden box.

Flipping to the pages she needed, she returned to her place next to him. With each address she read, he placed a small marker from the box onto the map. Once they finished, he sat back and motioned at the results.

"Look," he said.

Bella set the notes down, leaning forward. She pointed to two yellow markers. "These were the first fires?"

"*Dak*."

"And the second?"

He touched his finger near the green markers. "Here."

Bella pressed down on a yellow marker. "The Sizzle Show was first, and two weeks later," she moved to the second yellow circle, "Park View Inn is targeted. They're less than a block apart."

"Yes, every targeted curtain show house has a hotel nearby. By design or by coincidence, there's no denying the fires were started in pairs."

"Do you think the two weeks between are significant?" she asked, falling back into the cushions, arms crossed in thought.

"They must be to the arsonist. The pattern is fixed and hasn't deviated yet."

Sighing, Bella rubbed her forehead. "We are no closer to finding the culprit, and tomorrow is two weeks from the last fire."

"Let's see what we can find from other client logs. Maybe the same name will show up. We can tell the owners we're certain now specific businesses are being targeted. Once we have a list, we can discover where our mystery arsonist is scouting for the next fire."

THE CARRIAGE ROCKED, and the hushed clomp of horse hooves and rhythmic turn of wood over brick joined the rush of their heavy breaths within. Markus's feet braced on the opposite bench. His palms pressed to the low ceiling. Not to steady himself from the constant sway but to keep himself immobile while his wife had her delicious way with him. Every muscle bunched in an effort not to grab her and pound deep into her.

Sitting across from him, she'd become acutely aware of his struggle to keep his hands off her. While her scent had been lessening, allowing him more control than he'd managed in days, she was still an alluring temptation. Paired once again with the overt sexual setting of the curtain show houses they'd visited all evening and the occasional couple in a hurry to find the privacy of a hotel room, he'd been fighting a losing battle. And he hadn't been alone. Not a word was spoken, she'd climbed onto his lap, released his straining erection, and eased herself onto him, already wet and ready. He'd almost come, somehow gritting through the exhilaration of knowing she'd been just as desperate.

The silky length of her skirt flared out on either side of his parted thighs. Outside, the darkness of late night and the shifting, muted glow of street lamps allowed tantalizing glimpses of her beautiful face. A sensual flush darkened her cheeks. Her lips were swollen and glossy from his kisses. Her fingers alternated between kneading his shoulders to digging into the muscle, depending on how close she was to an orgasm. Markus's hips rolled, a gentle upward push to send her over the edge. Again. Her nails bit through his shirt, and he shuddered, relishing in the sensation of her pleasure arcing across their bond and her inner muscles working him.

Markus had to be careful. He'd rode her far too rough in the early hours of morning. At the time, he'd been mindless in his desire. In the knowledge of knowing he could *finally* sate his hunger when he needed her the most. The beast master had been unleashed, and there had been no rechaining. She was tender. Wisps of discomfort edged her release, a subtle reminder he couldn't ignore.

Curling his fingers into the wood above, his head fell back, and he surrendered. Hot pleasure erupted through his body, spilling out into her. One last powerful thrust sent him farther inside her, where another set of contractions milked his hard length. She cried out, burying her face in his neck, bending close. Markus clenched his jaw through the intense wave of gratification, like her, wanting to keep their moment as private as possible. When the last tremor of his climax faded, he panted, his arms collapsing at his side, his back sagging.

"Thank you," she whispered, kissing beneath his ear.

A little unsteady, he reached up and cupped the back of her head. The softness of her curls teased his palm. "Shouldn't I be saying that?"

"I've wanted you since I stepped out of the shower this morning, but I knew you'd say no." She lifted her head enough to kiss him. "You didn't this time."

"I couldn't," he confessed.

Her fingers fluttered across his cheek to his lips. "I know."

A part of him regretted she had no defense against his more primitive needs. In Ruthenia, partners knew what to expect. Being overcome by an ovulation phase wouldn't have the same impact with a pure-blooded mate. The chances of conception were low among his people. Bella's genetics were diluted, and Markus had no doubt she accepted the genetic material he'd had to offer with their first coupling in the alley. Everything else had just been him giving over to instinct and enjoying what the highly charged, erotic window allowed them.

Bella disengaged from him, wincing faintly as she swung her leg over his and sat between his feet. Reaching down, she picked up her messenger bag. After digging around inside, she pulled out a pair of panties. Her skirt bellowed upward as she shimmied into the underwear.

"That's a shame," he muttered, stuffing himself back into his pants.

She smiled at him. "They come off easily."

Lifting his hips, he pulled the edges of his fly back together, doing up the buttons. "Not any easier than going without."

She grimaced, adjusting her skirt back around her legs. "Not an option anymore."

No, because sex was magnificent but messy. And he, being the primal sort of male he was, couldn't help but grin at knowing she carried his seed within her. The carriage slowed to a stop, disrupting his naughty thoughts. Bella slung the bag across her chest and rechecked her clothes. Markus dropped his feet and twisted to look through the back window. He tapped the glass, catching Lunah's attention.

Stay where you're at when we stop, don't jump down right away.

He received a muffled yip in acknowledgment. Leaving his wolf home again hadn't been an option. Their bond demanded proximity. He could disregard the necessity on an infrequent basis. He was lucky the urgency to be with his mate had overridden Lunah's bond, or she'd have slept with them this morning. For their morning walk, she hadn't left his side to explore.

Brisk evening air swept into the cab. The driver, Hallen, bowed and moved to the side to allow them to exit. Markus had hired a carriage for the entire night, wanting to travel in clean comfort. The superior service was a bonus. He jumped down and helped Bella. The night breeze toyed with her skirt and short-sleeve silk tunic, giving him glimpses of the modest curves she always hid beneath loose clothes.

"Will you be long?" Hallen asked, holding on to the bottom of the driver's seat.

"Hopefully not," Markus answered, motioning for Lunah while pressing a hand to the small of Bella's back.

They'd visited The Enchanting Stage once, and the owner had been uncooperative. Markus had opted to drop the attempt to see the log book and visit other locations, returning to this one before they went home for the night.

"Excellent. I will pull up and wait near the corner."

"Thank you, Hallen."

The driver bowed again before climbing into the seat and easing down the road. Markus opened the red door for Bella and Lunah. A different woman than who'd greeted them earlier stood behind the welcome desk. She smiled in welcome and held out a card.

"Welcome to The Enchanting Stage, where all your fantasies are found. If you have any questions about our show lineup this evening, please don't hesitate to ask. We have rooms available for the Enchanted A and C stages. Please sign in here," she tapped a book, "and write in your preferred stage."

"Actually, we need to speak with Mr. Clarson, please," Markus said.

The woman blinked, seeming to see them for the first time. She took in Bella's conservative clothes, the wolf, and finally, Markus. Her gaze lingered on the braid hanging over his shoulder and the leather bracers wrapped around his wrists. She licked her lips and coiled her finger through the long blonde ponytail lying across her breast. Sheer, vibrant pink fabric draped from her shoulders to fall in a swoop to her navel. Her full breasts kept the material in place, along with a slender silver chain attached at her collarbone. Not much, but more than some wore in other curtain show houses.

"I will see if I can find him for you," she twittered, biting her bottom lip. "Is there anything else I can do?"

"No," Bella said.

The woman raised her brows and mouthed *okay*, turning around and disappearing through a bead curtain doorway. The pink and navy bead-glass screen tinkered back into position. Moments later, a short, balding man emerged. He scowled the second he spotted Markus.

"I thought I—"

"Everyone else has cooperated," Markus spoke over him. "We will examine the log in your presence and ask before we copy any information. We're looking for an arsonist, Mr. Clarson, not to cause any trouble for your clients."

"Viewers," Clarson corrected. "And I have

some, shall we say, patrons who are very powerful individuals."

"We aren't journalists. We're investigators," Markus reminded him, already having had this argument once before. "Please. We have the information from the other establishments. We're just trying to see if anything is similar."

Clarson drummed his fingers near the open logbook. "Very well. But I will watch everything, and you may only view the log three weeks before the event and none after."

"Deal," Markus said and motioned for Bella to do her research.

She already had her notebook pulled out and ready. Clarson turned to the page and then crossed his arms over his chest, his paunchy stomach distending, stretching the dark green shirt he wore.

Bella made quick work of the pages, flipping between the same two several times. "Look at this."

Markus and Clarson leaned closer.

Bella tapped her finger beneath a loopy penned name. "This person, Allie Bertmeum, visited five times in the two weeks before the fire and was present the night of the fire. She also checked into Haven Star Hotel the night of their fire."

"She is your suspect?" Clarson asked, eyes wide.

"She did not visit any other establishments," Bella said carefully. "It's an interesting coincidence. May I copy her name and dates?"

Clarson nodded and pushed the book closer. "Yes, please. This person has not returned, so I have nothing to protect."

A frantic scream echoed from the main corridor leading to the stages. Sounds of chaos ensued. Lunah lowered her front paws and snarled.

Sickness, the bad sickness! she frantically conveyed across their bond.

Markus's heart lurched. He grabbed Bella's elbow and propelled her toward the door. She made a hasty grab for her notebook, the pen she'd been holding flying off somewhere.

"Hey!" she squealed. "What in the inhabited world, Markus?"

"HRS," he stated, shoving open the door. "Get Hallen to take you to the nearest enforcement radio and call for a containment unit. Now."

"But—"

"No argument, Bella," he pleaded.

She searched his face, her fear an uncomfortable prickle across his nerves. "Please be careful."

"Do not set foot back inside this building," he ordered. He pressed a hard kiss to her lips. "I love you, now go."

Markus didn't give her the chance to respond, sending her the rest of the way through the doorway. Clarson blinked behind the counter.

"You have an HRS incident on your property," Markus informed him. "Bella has gone to call a containment unit."

"What? That's impossible and ridiculous," the owner sputtered. "How can you possibly know that?"

Markus motioned to Lunah. "She's already scented the disease."

Clarson's face went sheet white, and he whimpered, his gaze darting between the main hall and the front door. Markus glared and pointed. "Don't you dare abandon your business."

"B-but, there's, it's a, I'm not," the owner whined incoherently, his hands moving in wild, jerky motions.

"Is there another exit?" Markus asked, unsheathing the knife he always kept at his back.

"T-two." Clarson indicated to the left and right. "One behind Stage C and the other behind Stage F."

Damn it. People had likely already fled through those exits. Trying to force others to stay by blocking the front door would only create a mad rush to unguarded exits. Only the infected could be his concern, not the other patrons.

Lunah, straes'ya, Markus commanded, and she immediately obeyed, hunting her prey.

Markus followed, pushing past the frantic and terrified rush of men and a few women. Lunah made several random turns. The corridors wrapped around each stage, creating a maze effect. Lunah came to a sudden stop, and Markus did the same, his attention drawn to the idle figure twitching in the center of an aisle. When no victims were sensed, a human rabies syndrome infected tended to conserve energy until a new target appeared. The animated stage was very short, anywhere from fifteen minutes to two hours. Most two-hour cases were in containment facilities, where the infected did little more than stand idle in a room with no victims. This zombie-like human had at least ten more minutes of stolen energy left.

Blood smeared down a nearby wall and puddled on the floor beneath a partially closed door. The woman's head jerked to the right, causing the updo atop her head to bob. Her bloody fingers twitched. An eerie, growly snarl filled the hall. Markus took a calming breath, drawing on years of adrenaline saturated missions.

Lunah, voztrikat, he ordered, then added, *but do not allow contact.*

The wolf zoomed past the diseased woman, providing a necessary yet dangerous distraction. Not knowing the difference between human and animal any longer, the woman flew forward, the virus giving her inhuman speed. Lunah reacted, barking, and dodged in the opposite direction, spinning. The woman followed, and Markus had his first look at her.

Pink, frothy drool coated her chin and dribbled down her neck to saturate the front of her blood-soaked shirt. The once cheery yellow fabric was a garish nightmare. Blood splattered the front of her sky-blue skirt and soaked the hem. She'd managed to kill at least one person, probably the poor soul who'd bled out in the curtain room. The trail of blood on the wall and a line of drops soaking into the light gray carpet going the opposite direction from the smeared wallpaper told him she'd likely managed to bite two additional victims.

Lunah snapped, fled, woofed, and bolted, keeping the infected in constant motion, edging her closer to Markus. Shifting his weight onto the balls of his feet, Markus waited for the right second to act. Every bodily fluid in the woman was now contaminated and carried the active virus. Knife poised to slash, Markus spun to the left as Lunah kept the infected's attention to the right. The blade sliced cleanly across the exposed back of her neck, severing the spinal cord. Her body crumbled to the floor, her teeth gnashing. Lunah bounced into the air and landed feet away, safe from the snapping jaws. Markus sagged against the nearest wall, careful to keep the knife's edge facing out.

Scared, Bella is scared, Lunah whined.

Tell her all is well and ask if the containment unit is on the way.

She has radioed them, she has. She does not know when they will arrive, she does not.

Markus sighed and stared at the woman,

who, unable to see Lunah any longer, had gone back to being still, only the occasional snap of her teeth letting him know the virus still animated an otherwise dead body. Such a waste. All for a moment of pleasure. He wondered if her lover was the one deceased in the room or if the individual had been about to become her lover, and others were infected in the city, spreading the sickness. While not as prevalent as it once had been, thanks to the encouragement of committed relationships, HRS still managed to be a deadly concern.

No one else ventured down the corridor, the silence all-encompassing. Markus straightened, deciding to check for anyone hiding or other victims. A search yielded no wounded. The body in the private curtain room had bled out from a bite to the neck. Common for the first attack, where the infected was alone with the victim and focused. The others tended to happen faster, with distractions that allowed for bite and release versus bite and gnaw.

Urgent voices echoed through the corridors. Markus motioned for Lunah to come to his side. His wolf could be jarring to an already stressed team. Moments later, four people eased around the corner with restraint poles ready. They sagged in noticeable relief when they saw the infected already handled.

"Any other victims?" a short, blonde woman asked.

Markus indicated to the blood on the wall

and floor. "I think at least two, but they must have fled with the rest of the crowd."

"Great," a man muttered, dropping the end of his pole to the floor. "We'll be chasing down two incidents in two weeks if they don't turn themselves in."

"We'll make sure we talk to whoever shows up to report this for the papers, urging the bitten to check in to the quarantine facility," the blonde replied. "That's all we can do unless they're waiting for us." Her attention snapped to Markus. "Were you bitten, or did you come in contact with any fluids?"

"No, neither of us did. We were careful."

The woman seemed to notice Lunah for the first time, flinching back when her gaze landed on the wolf. The man standing behind her hugged his pole to his chest.

"Beast master," the pole hugger whispered.

Lunah's soft growl made them all stumble back. "If we're finished?"

The blonde nodded. "Yes, of course. Th-thank you for helping."

Markus nodded and went in the opposite direction of the unit, searching as Lunah led the way out for the two additional victims.

Do you scent anyone else? Any more bad sickness?

No, I do not, no.

Markus quickened his steps, not comfortable knowing two possible infected were outside with his mate. Granted, they weren't contagious for the next two weeks unless they were intimate with someone, but that sane knowledge didn't decrease his anxiety. The crowd was thick outside, everyone straining to glimpse the event. Haven City Enforcement had set up a roped barricade and had created a corridor from the alley to the containment unit's cart, where the dealt with infected would be placed. Markus ignored the hum of the crowd, searching over the congestion and street for a familiar horse and driver.

To the left, Bella is to the left, Lunah instructed, pressing through the crowd, which separated like torn paper for the massive wolf. She danced and yipped.

The carriage came into view. Bella leaned out the door, waving the moment she spotted him. Lunah set her paws on the floor of the cab.

Vye! Markus snapped, his heart launching into his throat. *Do not lick. Do not touch. Back of the carriage, now.*

Lunah's tail tucked between her legs, and she sank away from Bella, who frowned, reaching for the wolf. Lunah darted out of her reach and leaped onto the rack on the rear.

"Do not touch either of us," Markus instructed, stopping before her. "Do you have a scarf or anything I can use to wrap around my knife?"

She tossed her messenger bag away and then grabbed at her skirt. When the fabric didn't give, she ducked inside. The muffle of a conversation sounded. She returned in the doorway, a small pocket knife in hand. "How much?"

Markus clenched his jaw. He didn't want her to destroy her beautiful silk skirt. Setting the knife on the ground, he peeled his shirt off. Using the shirt, he picked up the knife and bunched the fabric around the contaminated blade.

She nibbled on her bottom lip before disappearing into the cab. Markus instructed the driver to take them home. Inside the carriage, he kept himself small. Bundled shirt and hands pressed between his knees. Shoulders hunched.

"I'm glad you're safe," Bella's quiet words floated to him.

"I'm sorry you were scared."

"Of course, I was scared. You are my world, Markus. I just found you. I can't lose you."

CHAPTER

NINE

STEAM CURLED IN THE AIR, FILLING THE BATHROOM with humidity and the scent of a forest. Bella squeezed another handful of soap onto Markus's waiting palm. He rubbed the cleanser between his hands and scrubbed the bubbles through Lunah's thick fur. The wolf licked at his chin, her eyes blinking from the water splashing around them. This was the second time he'd washed her after washing himself twice. Bella knew once was enough, but fear of the virus ran deep.

She set the bottle on the counter behind her and picked up a huge, fluffy towel. After Markus rinsed Lunah and shut off the water, she handed him first a towel for the wolf, then one for himself. She finished drying Lunah, the good girl stepping onto a towel and sitting patiently while Bella rubbed over every inch of fur. Markus wrapped a towel around his waist and draped another over his shoulders.

"I'll take care of her," Bella said, massaging

the towel over Lunah's shoulders and behind her ears. "Go, start the fire, check on your knife."

He nodded and disappeared through the bedroom. Bella rested her head against Lunah's back, inhaling the familiar scent of her husband's soap. They'd spoken hardly a word since arriving at the apartment. Markus had instructed her to leave the door open and open the woodstove. Out in the corridor, uncaring about any show he may give the one other resident who'd purchased a unit on their floor or her mother if she opted to investigate their late arrival, he'd stripped. Everything, from his shoes to his belt, had been shoved into the stove. His knife and the rings he always wore had been placed in a disinfecting solution in the kitchen sink, and the shirt balled up with the rest of the items to be burned. He and Lunah had then gone to the shower while Bella handled everything needing to be touched. They'd worked in silent unison. A team. With each bubble that had swirled down the drain, her anxiety level had dropped. They were safe.

Bella settled Lunah outside before searching out Markus. She found him sitting on the floor in the front tef the woodstove, poking at the cinders of fabric and slower burning leather. The faint glow of amber drew attention to the hard lines of his face set in an intense frown. Stopping behind him, she slid her fingers through his damp hair.

"Are you all right?" she asked softly.

He placed the poker back in the holder and closed the woodstove. "*Dak*, I'm fine."

Rising, he took her hand and led her back to the bedroom. Bella tried to decipher his emotions to determine whether he was indeed *fine*. Only a trace of anxiety lingered, having flared the hardest when Lunah had attempted to touch her at the scene. He'd been closed off since, making her wonder if he'd shut her out again. She didn't have the energy to argue with him if he had, also figuring at times they deserved privacy. The ability to sever their connection wasn't one she possessed, but she doubted Markus constantly monitored her emotional state. If he wasn't sharing, she had to trust he didn't want any input from her, either.

Exhausted, Bella barely managed to undress and shuffle to the dresser to pull out a thin, chemise-style nightgown. The pale blue silk slid over her, a cool relief for her adrenaline heated skin. Markus slipped outside, leaving the glass door open. Fresh, chilly air wafted inside, fluttering her nightgown. Bella crawled underneath the covers, dousing the only lit lamp.

Minutes later, the blankets shifted, and the mattress depressed on her right side. His arm banded around her waist, tugging her close, curling around her. Although an erection pressed into her thigh, he made no move to seduce. He nuzzled her shoulder and rested his cheek on her bicep. Beneath the covers, he worked the bottom of her nightgown over her hips to bunch beneath her navel. His palm splayed wide across her bare, low abdomen. And then he stilled.

Bella wrapped her fingers around his wrist as love and possession threatened to overwhelm her. Nothing could happen to this man. Nothing could take him from her. With one simple gesture, he'd acknowledged and protected the spark of life possibly growing within her womb.

Their future beneath his hand.

Part of her wished they'd had more time to learn each other before they learned to be parents, but another part couldn't wait to hold the proof of their love. If she were pregnant. Nervousness danced in her stomach, along with doubt. When the moment came, she'd handle the outcome then. For now, she'd enjoy the quiet solitude with her husband.

Morning brought the passion Markus had denied himself when they'd fallen asleep. A desire she'd been all too ready to fulfill. His mouth bit and licked her neck, his fingers laced with hers, and his body moved in a perfect rhythm over hers. Only once he had her crying incoherent sounds did he relent, bringing them both to an intense release.

Bella freed her hands and hugged his broad shoulders, burying her face in his neck, slick with sweat. "Can we stay here for the rest of the day? Just like this?"

He sighed and lifted above her. Gently, he

brushed damp curls from her face. His golden eyes searched hers. Still buried deep within her, his every movement, no matter how small, brought attention to their joining. "Someone is going to start a fire tonight, and we're no closer to discovering who than we were three days ago."

Her morning-addled and orgasm-fogged brain tried to bring forward some important fact she thought she'd discovered before the HRS incident. But the thought was illusive, and she groaned in frustration. "I need a shower and some coffee so I can think."

Grunting, he pushed off and rolled into a stand from the bed. "I'll get your coffee while you get a shower."

She lifted onto her elbows. "No shower for you?"

Heat filled his gaze as he looked her over. "After you're out."

The urge to tease him emboldened her, and she trailed her fingers down her stomach toward her spread legs. "Are you sure?"

Jaw clenched, he pointed a finger at her. "Stop tempting. Shower, now. Then tell me about this thought I know you had."

She stuck out her tongue and huffed. "Fine. But when this is over—"

"*Dak*, an entire day. No argument from me."

• • •

Buttoning his pants, Markus rolled his shoulders and sniffed to try to ease the fog of morning away. He needed a shower, too, but the coffee first would have to suffice. Brushing his fingers through his tangled hair, he failed to realize he wasn't alone.

"Good morning. Well, technically, it's afternoon. Are you two having to work nights for this case?" Madeleine asked, leaning against the kitchen counter and blowing into a steaming mug.

Fingers stuck mid-motion in his hair, Markus froze. He was half-dressed and smelled like sex. Probably looked like that's all he'd been doing, too. Damn it. What to do...

"I didn't expect you," Markus admitted.

Madeleine smiled and motioned to the stove. "I'm off today. Coffee?"

"*Dak*, please."

She turned and brought down two cups. "Don't be embarrassed. You're newly married and in a healthy relationship. I'm not at all bothered. I *do* admit I miss my husband, but that is my problem. I seem to miss him more each year I'm without him."

Markus blew out a long breath. "I do not mean to disrespect you."

"Why would you think you are?" she asked, setting the pot back on the stove.

He motioned to his bare torso.

She spooned sugar into both mugs. "This is your home too, Markus. Now, about this case. Long nights?"

Markus accepted one of the cups and added some milk. "We're investigating fires started at hotels and curtain show houses."

Madeleine made a face. "Those houses… nothing good comes of going into one."

"You will get no argument from me," Markus murmured, sipping his beverage.

"I'm sure any number of people could think of reasons to burn one of those show houses to the ground," Madeleine said, leaning back against the counter and taking the cup in both hands.

"We came to the same conclusion," Markus admitted. "But the hotel fires are causing a bit of trouble. They're linked, but we don't know how."

"I had an idea about that," Bella said from behind.

Markus glanced over his shoulder. She'd dressed in a thin maroon knit sweater with a draping neckline and ochre pants. A braided belt of navy, ochre, and maroon drew attention to her slender waist, while the rest of the clothing only hinted at the modest curves beneath. Her drying curls were loose around her shoulders, a rarity. Before they left for the evening, she'd have them styled into a bun or clipped into place at the nape of her neck. Only on rare occasions did she pull the sides back, leaving the rest in glorious disarray. When dry, her dark curls were thick and wild. Like everything else about her, he loved them.

She stopped at his side, and he coiled one

of the ringlets around his finger, leaning down and kissing her. Her hand slid around to his back, her fingers pressing into the muscles until her nails bit. A shiver of need raced along his spine. Markus wanted to back her up, lift her onto the counter, and settle between her thighs. He wanted to shove his hand down her pants and discover....

Growling, he tore his mouth free and leaned close, whispering into her ear, "My turn in the shower."

Her wicked fingers pressed between their body, dancing over the waistband of his pants until she discovered his erection nearly pushing free. "Not fair," she breathed against his jaw.

Pulling back, he was careful not to face his mother-in-law in his current condition. "Thanks for the coffee, Madeleine. I'll be back out in a few."

"Don't take too long," Bella groused. "I want to get started on this research."

He swept past, keeping the words he wanted to say to himself. No, he wouldn't take long at all. All he had to do was recall any one of their recent bouts of intimacy, including this morning, and he'd be finished. He went to the shower, stepping free of his pants and under the water before it heated completely. Panting, he dropped his forehead to the tile and wondered how in the arctic he was going to handle time away from her when he couldn't manage more than a couple of hours now.

Not well, he imagined.

After quickly washing, he dressed in fresh clothes and collected his wolf. She'd need to go for a walk soon, but Markus wanted to know what Bella may have discovered. They were out of time. Markus doubted they'd find the culprit in time to prevent the fire. The best he could hope for now was to discover the culprit before he had to leave the country.

Brushing his damp hair, he found both the women in the living room. The cup of coffee he'd abandoned waited for him on the table, steaming, which meant it'd been refreshed. He wasn't picky, he didn't mind drinking cold coffee, but he appreciated the kindness. At the couch, he sat on the floor in front of the table and held the brush over his shoulder. Bella scooted until he sat between her legs, the weight of his hair lifting as she pulled all the strands together. The brush disappeared from his fingers. Braiding his hair was an affection they both enjoyed.

"Tell me what you think you've found," he said, reaching for the coffee.

"The second set of curtain show house and hotel fires had the same visitor's name appear. While the third set had a different name, there was a common visitor on those logs as well. Each set of fires had a corresponding visitor to *both* establishments," she said, her fingers scraping across his scalp to his neck.

Markus swallowed a groan. "But each set had a different common visitor?"

"Yes, but it's weird. All the letters are the same," she said.

Markus frowned. "What do you mean?"

"Look there, I wrote them all down in a row."

Keeping his head still, he reached for the open notebook. "We don't know the visitor for the first fire because everything was destroyed, correct?"

"Correct. However, after looking back through the logs, I think I found what the name would have been. Like I said, the letters are all the same."

Markus looked over the page. "Anagrams."

"I believe so."

"They're all female names." He tapped the paper. "That means we're looking for a woman."

"So, an anagram of her name or someone else's?"

Markus considered the limited evidence they'd collected so far, along with their personal experiences. He turned to a new page in her notebook and grabbed a pen. "The first fire was right before we left for Thanzia."

"Yes."

"And what were the roads like two weeks before that?" he asked. "I know government buildings were still closed except for critical personnel. What about businesses?"

"Businesses open the moment customers begin showing up at doors," Madeleine said.

"Some open sooner than others. Hotels never really close."

"But the curtain show houses?" Markus asked, glancing across at her.

Madeleine shrugged. "I can't speak from experience, but I'd imagine after a long, boring winter, many who go to them regularly are desperate to take in a show. You'd have to ask an owner, but I bet they open as soon as an Icekutian can wade a carriage through the snow."

Icekutians were the only horse breed capable of withstanding the arctic temperatures of late fall into mid-spring. Only a handful of people could afford them, let alone maintain a carriage business utilizing the regal breed.

Markus turned to the list of curtain show houses. "We won't ever know what type of establishment The Sizzle Show was, but these other curtain houses? Most of them are what I'd consider higher end."

"All the shows are a luxury," Madeleine stated, holding her arms out. "They're an indulgence only those on this side of the Everflow River can really afford."

"Even the curtain shows near The Rows?" Markus asked.

Madeleine nodded. "Even those. The rent might be cheaper, but the performances are not."

"The wealthy come to ogle as the poor subjugate themselves," Bella sneered.

Markus turned a page, reading over her

notes. "And become wealthy off the eyes of their viewers. Don't forget C.G. said his wife is able to purchase an apartment in this building. She has made enough on the stage to provide a better life for herself. You can't fault that."

"No, but I don't have to like it," she said, petulance saturating her voice.

"How many affairs do you think happen in one of those places?" Markus asked.

"Actual affairs or quick liaisons with a sex hustler?" Bella asked.

He turned, bracing his elbow on her thigh. "Do you think many of those sex hustlers go to a hotel?"

Nibbling on her bottom lip, she considered his question and slowly shook her head. "No. I think whatever they're willing to do happens either in a room or in an alley nearby."

Markus nodded and shifted back toward the table. "I agree."

"You're thinking someone had an affair?" Madeleine asked.

"I'm thinking," Markus drew out, "the time adds up for an HRS incident that someone is avenging."

Bella gasped and snatched the book from his hand. "Every two weeks!"

"*Dak.*"

Madeleine tapped her chin. "And they met their lover at a curtain show but had an actual affair at a hotel?"

"Contracting human rabies syndrome, either from a single unfaithful lover or because they took multiple lovers from the shows," Markus said. "I think it fits."

"We never thought to look at the HRS victim lists," Bella sighed.

"Why would we? We weren't investigating the origins of an outbreak. We were investigating fires. The motive could have been anything."

Madeleine lifted a finger. "I can help with that."

Markus glanced at Bella, who made an I-don't-know face and lifted her hands. She wrapped her arms around his shoulders and rested her chin atop his head while they waited. Markus threaded his fingers through one of her hands. Lunah stood, stretched, groaned, and plopped down at his side, rolling onto her back, paws curled, exposing her belly. Markus didn't need their connection to know she was ready for her walk.

"Soon," he whispered, rubbing her belly. She shimmied back and forth, groaning again.

Madeleine hurried into the living room, a binder in her hand. "Here you are." She stopped and stared down at Lunah, laughing. "Oh my."

"She needs to go for her walk," Markus said, accepting the binder. "What's this?"

"I'm a couple's therapist and a match-maker. I can't afford to have any of my couples show up on an HRS list, so I monitor them closely. If one does happen to show up, I learn what went wrong, and if in future sessions or pairings, those same situations manifest, I know to either advise against a contract or caution the couple I'm guiding," Madeleine explained. "I've only had two clients show up on the list, and that was over two decades ago. A sad situation I learned much from." She motioned at the book. "All the lists from this year are in the front."

Markus opened the binder. Pages and pages of cut and pasted newspaper clippings filled the ringed book. Markus positioned the case on his bent knees and searched for dates.

"I'll take Lunah on her walk if you'd like," Madeleine said.

Markus looked up, brows raised. "That'd be great, thank you."

"Of course, I enjoy taking her." Madeleine snapped her fingers and patted her leg. "Come on, pretty girl, let's go enjoy the summer afternoon."

Lunah hopped up, yipped, and pranced around Madeleine. Seemed his wolf enjoyed walking with Bella's mother, too. The two left, the door closing quietly behind them.

Bella leaned over his shoulder, her curls catching on his beard. She touched under a line of text. "Look here, March 16th, there were three incidents. Two women and a man."

Markus placed her notes on top of the clippings. He read the names she'd singled out, "Amelie Tumbler, Emelia Tumbrel, Ambrite Lemuel, Allie Bertmeum..."

"Those all match with the letters from the

man who died, Emmet Brieulla," she whispered. "That's it. That's why the fires are being set. Emmet took one or more lovers from a curtain show house, and look, he died at Park View Inn."

"He must have frequented The Sizzle Show, which was why those two businesses were set on fire first."

"Why keep going?" she asked.

"Maybe destroying those properties wasn't enough. Didn't accomplish what she wanted, so she's kept going," Markus theorized. "We won't know for sure until we catch her."

"We know what to look for now, at least," Bella sighed.

Markus closed both books and set them on the table. "Come on, we need to search the books of all the curtain show houses we can that haven't been targeted yet. Maybe we'll get lucky and prevent the fire from being set tonight."

TEN

"SHE'S BEEN HERE, TOO," BELLA WHISPERED, turning the sign-in log for Markus to view. "Emelita Lumber."

He braced both arms on the wide counter and hung his head. "How many anagrams can one name make?"

"As many as she needs, I'm guessing," Bella said, keeping her voice low. "This is the third curtain show house she's visited in the past two weeks."

Markus grasped her elbow and pulled her across the room. Bella's heart thundered in her ears. They were so very close, and yet knew nothing about the woman, except she used fake names and started fires.

"Did she visit tonight?" he asked.

Bella shook her head. "She hasn't visited any of them tonight. Not yet. What do you want to do?"

He pinched the bridge of his nose. "I need

somewhere to think that won't require us to keep a curtain open."

Bella took his hand and led him outside into the cool night. The same driver from the previous evening waited at the curb. Lunah sat inside, her muzzle sticking out the open window. Her entire head popped out when she scented them. The carriage sat next to a street lamp and would provide the perfect quiet space for him to plan their next move.

Inside, Bella settled across from him and petted between Lunah's ears.

"Can I see your notes, please?" he asked.

Bella handed him her notebook. He leaned toward the wash of light. The quiet rustle of pages flipping and Lunah's occasional muzzle lick were the only sound for several minutes.

"If we have all the relevant information, she visited each business twice and the one that eventually burned a third time, usually the night before setting the fire," he said.

"So, four times total for the one she damaged." Bella rested her elbows on her knees. "Has she been to one of them three times recently?"

"*Vye*, but this is the first time she's targeted three curtain show houses. Tonight is two weeks from Mr. Weldon's hotel fire. If she stays on that pattern, she will start a fire." He turned a page and tapped the book. "She *did* visit Midnight Meetings last night." He snapped the book closed and returned it. "I think that'll be our best chance of finding her."

"And C.G.'s wife is there," Bella said, stuffing the notebook into the bag. "She can help us."

Twisting, she knocked on the window to get Hallen's attention. She slid the window open and gave him instructions. Seconds later, the carriage jerked into motion. The ride to Midnight Meetings was only a few blocks away. The sights were familiar. Destitution. Streets too narrow and lined with small homes too close together. A fire in The Row's devasted if not caught in time.

Markus had rescued her from the depths of such poverty, plucking her from a dilapidated rental deep within The Row's to a top-floor apartment where only the wealthy could afford to reside. She still found herself in disbelief over her change of circumstances. His touch brushed over her hand and then captured her fingers within his. Bella jumped at the contact, yanked from memories.

"You won't go back," he whispered, bringing her hand to his lips. "Never."

"I know." Because that would mean something terrible had happened to him. A situation that didn't bear thinking about.

The carriage rolled to a stop a few doors down from the curtain show house. Two other carriages were waiting for passengers to exit. A sense of urgency rode. Markus grasped the handle first and motioned for Lunah to hop out. He climbed down, watched the street for a moment, and then reached for her hand.

Bella smiled. "The arsonist burns inside a building. She hasn't done anything violent."

"True, and I wasn't worried about her." He rubbed Lunah's ears. "Lunah says all smells fine so far. She's going with us since we'll be moving beyond the foyer."

That he'd be taking no chances was left unspoken. Bella slid her fingers through his and pulled his arm tight to her body. He leaned down and gave her a quick kiss. A man with two snickering women on his arms stumbled toward the curtain show house door. Another two men joined them, one of them wrapping his arm around the waist of a woman and swinging her away from the man and into his body. She laughed harder, wrapping herself around him.

Bella rolled her eyes. "I wonder if they offer group rooms."

"I wonder if any of them bothered to read the paper this morning," Markus stated, glaring.

"There's a reason HRS is still around," Bella sighed while they waited for the riotous group to disappear inside. Bella wondered if one of the women was their mysterious arsonist or if she'd arrive alone.

Two more men slipped inside behind the group, their heads hung low, their clothing nondescript. The carriages ambled away, their wheels clacking over brick.

"Ready?" Markus asked, squeezing her hand.

"Ready."

Inside, the group was being led away, their exuberance echoing down the corridor. One of the two men was signing in, and a hostess waited with a smile. When he finished, she took his arm and guided him behind a thick curtain. A new woman slid into her position and motioned to the sign-in log. Behind the counter, a hostess leaned forward, pressing her breasts over the top of the corset top. A sheer pink swath of fabric barely covered her rear.

"One room or two?" she asked.

"Actually," Markus said, stepping up to the counter. "We were hoping to speak to Willow."

"Willow is performing on stage nine. She has..." The woman sidled over to a different logbook and ran her finger down the page. "One room available for reservation for her next performance. Would you like her stage?"

"We need to find out when someone signs in tonight for a room," Markus said.

The woman straightened. "I'm sorry, we can't disclose any of our patrons."

"We know," Bella said, pressing a hand down and leaning closer to the woman to whisper. "You know of the fires in the other curtain show houses?"

The woman nodded.

"We think the arsonist may be here tonight. If I show you a name, can you tell me when she arrives?" Bella asked. "That's all we're asking."

"A-all right, sure." The hostess glanced at

the pair leaving the foyer. After they disappeared down the corridor, she moved to the sign-in log and picked up the pen. She glanced at Bella expectantly.

"Emelita Lumber will be the name she signs in with," Bella said.

The woman's hand froze over the log. Color fled her cheeks. Markus pulled his hand free from Bella's and moved to the check-in book.

"What is it?" he asked.

"She's here already," the hostess whispered, her trembling hand touching the page. "She's in room seven for stage ten."

"May we go there?" Markus asked, his voice pitched low and urgent.

"Please, yes. What should I do? Should I do anything? Tell the owner? My manager?"

"Let's make sure she's in the room first," Markus said. "If she's not there, we'll have worried everyone for nothing."

"Right." She nodded and smoothed her hands down the front of her corset. "Okay. I will show you the room."

Midnight Meeting's was set up with a central aisle reaching all ten stages with smaller halls leading to the surrounding private viewing rooms. The gold in the damask wallpaper gleamed in the muted light of red glass lanterns. The thick navy carpet softened their steps. A quarter of the way down, Markus slammed an arm out, forcing Bella to stop.

"Lunah scents smoke," he said.

Chills broke out across her skin. The sense

of urgency turned into an outright pressure to find the arsonist. To stop her before she could cause any more damage. Maybe she'd just lit the match. Or touched a flame to an object. Whatever the cause of the smoke, the fire had yet to truly start. At least, Bella hoped.

Bella grabbed Markus's sleeve. "The private entrance."

"Can the private entrance be used as an exit?" Markus asked the hostess. "Or is there a fire exit near stage ten?"

"The fire exit is behind stage five," she said, turning toward the right and pointing. "Why? What's happening?"

"Where's a water shot?"

"Um." The hostess twisted her hands and blinked. "I'm not certain. Perhaps...." She blew out a hard breath and shook her head. "I'm not sure, I don't know, I'm sorry."

"Find the manager now and let them know a fire has been started and to begin the evacuation process," Markus told her and then turned to Bella, grabbing both her upper arms. "Please go to the exit behind stage five, make sure she doesn't—"

"Willow," Bella interrupted, grabbing his forearms. "Willow is on stage nine."

Frustration and a hint of fear bloomed across their bond. Bella squeezed his arms and stared up at him. She could see the internal fight to keep her safe yet allow her to help.

A hard glint sparked in his golden eyes. "If anything happens to you...."

"Find who started the fire. Don't let her escape. I will find Willow and ask her where the water shot is, and we'll get out." She pressed her fingers harder into his muscled forearms. "I promise."

He searched her gaze for a second longer and then nodded. After pressing a hard kiss to her lips, he and Lunah raced down the hall. The hostess flapped her hands and stared after them.

"The manager, go now!" Bella ordered. "Tell whoever is in charge to get all the water shots to stage ten."

A hint of smoke drifted in the air. Concerned voices sounded behind the nearest drawn curtains to the private rooms. Bella ignored the half-dressed or those stuffing themselves back into clothes as they yanked open curtains to investigate. She ran to stage nine and searched for a door instead of a curtain, the way Willow would get into her performance area. A narrow panel with a small hole shoulder height caught her attention. Bella wedged her finger into the hole, and the panel folded open.

Weak candlelight flickered, reflecting off the glass panes of the viewing rooms. Bella stepped into the room. The panel snapped shut. On the center of the stage, Willow writhed, sheer fabric sliding and shifting around and beneath her nude body. Bella kept her attention on the woman's face, not wanting to experience any part of the erotic show she was performing. A faint haze of smoke filled the air.

Bella stayed near the wall and cupped her hands, whispering, "Willow, psst, Willow."

Willow froze, her body turned toward Bella. "Wh—"

Smoke curled along the ceiling and created a faint haze in the room. Bella gasped and coughed. "We have to leave!"

"A fire!" Willow scrambled from the stage, clutching gossamer fabric to her body. She fell to her knees, searching the floor. "Where's my... where's my robe?"

Bella tried to see anything on the dark carpeted floor. She inched deeper into the room and swept her foot around. "Where did you drop it?"

Someone knocked on the glass. Willow stood and waved her arms. "There is a fire! Get out!"

A heavy thump vibrated through the walls, and glass trembled. Bella glanced over her shoulder and bit her lip. The scent of smoke grew more pungent, making each breath burn. "We need to go."

"All right, forget the robe. They've all seen me naked anyway, right?" Willow said, her laughter hitched and weak.

Sympathy had Bella grabbing a curtain within reach. Running out of a burning building naked was an indignity she wouldn't make the woman bear. She yanked at the thick fabric. The drape didn't budge. Bella grasped the velvet in both hands and pulled. A creak and a groan sounded before the material tore free. "Here, we can use this."

Willow took the torn drape and wrapped it around her like a towel. Bella undid her belt and handed the braided cord to the performer. After securing the makeshift clothes, Willow led the way to the panel. Willow pushed and tried tugging the small hole, but the pane didn't budge.

"It's stuck," Willow said, yanking in another direction to dislodge the panel.

Bella squeezed her eyes closed and gritted her teeth. *Of course,* the way out had been jammed. *Of course,* they were trapped in a room surrounded by sheets of glass while a fire burned nearby. "Is there another exit?"

Willow continued to strain to open the panel. "No. This is it. Unless we can break a viewing window."

Bella spun around, searching the small area for anything useful. Useless glass pleasure toys and silk scarves littered the floor and low stage. A folded chair lay near the platform. Bella went to grab the chair. Smoke thickened the air, limiting the visibility in the room. Her eyes stung, and she tried to blink away the discomfort. Another cough wracked her body, her lungs burning for clean air. Gripping the top of the chair to use the thicker legs on the glass, Bella swung with all her might at the nearest window. The wood cracked and bounced in her hands. The glass held.

"Damn it," she whispered and broke into another coughing fit.

Willow also heaved and choked on smoke. "Why did you come for me?"

Bella swung the chair again. "I couldn't." Another hard whack. "Leave you."

"But you don't even know me," the woman whispered behind her.

Short of breath, the chair drooped in Bella's hold as she gasped and swallowed against the air deprived of oxygen. "I know C.G. He's a friend, and he cares about you. I couldn't let his wife die in a fire, not when I knew where you were."

"But now you're—"

"No. No negative thoughts," Bella wheezed out. "My husband..." She swallowed and coughed again. "My mate won't allow any-thing to happen to us, okay?"

Bella lifted the chair and tried to smack it against the glass, but weakened by the air quality, the furniture just bounced again. Willow took the chair from her limp fingers and heaved it upward, slamming it into the window, screaming.

"Break, damn it!" Willow shouted, bashing the chair into the glass until a leg busted free, flying at Bella and slicing across her cheek. "I can't... I have to get out of here! *Break*!"

Bella shielded her face from another wood fragment. The chunk scraped across her fore-arm. Bella grabbed at the mangled chair before Willow could do any more damage. "Stop! The glass isn't going to break. The chair isn't strong enough."

A sob tore from Willow. She hunched into herself, her arms hugging her waist. "I can't die in here, I can't!"

Bella would have sighed in exasperation if she'd been able. Instead, she wrapped her arms around the other woman and pulled her to the spot she figured was furthest from the fire. The thick smoke obscured the other side of the room and the ceiling. Bella laid on the floor and urged Willow to do the same.

"It's easier to breathe down here, come on," Bella said, tugging the curtain around Willow.

Another sob left the woman as she sank to the floor next to Bella. She grabbed for Bella's hand. "I had everything planned, you know? M-my whole—" A cough cut through her words. She took a long, deep breath. "My whole future."

"With C.G.?" Bella asked quietly.

Willow sniffled. "If that's what he wanted. I'd hoped maybe, you know, he'd be different about my lineage. Or lack of. Marrying a Fane-line for a year is acceptable, but not any longer." She turned her head away and coughed. "C.G. says he never marries anyone longer, so I knew if he decided not to stay, it wasn't because of who I am, but who he is. I'd hoped, though... I love him."

"Have you," Bella coughed, "told him?"

"No." She sobbed again. "But I should have."

Taking a breath hurt, and the first sliver of fear stabbed at Bella. She tried to stay calm, but the air burned her eyes, her nose, her throat, and panic blossomed.

Bella, my Bella! Coming, we are coming!

Tears escaped from her closed eyes and ran across her nose and cheeks to drip to the floor. She wished the communication with Lunah went both ways like Markus could do, but she hadn't figured out how to speak to the wolf unless she was sitting in front of her. Determination and alarm flared across her bond.

Markus.

Either the situation with the fire was bad enough for him to be scared, or her fear was affecting him. Or a combination of both. Bella didn't want him distracted by her anxiety. She tried to calm her frayed nerves, but the tears kept falling. The smoke continued to grow thicker.

"Markus, hurry," she whispered.

MARKUS SHOVED the arsonist at the Haven City enforceman. Flames licked out the back windows into the narrow alley where the private entrance/exit was located. The enforceman reached out to brace the woman before she tripped over her layered skirt. Red over dark blue, both tied, one easily discarded. She also wore two shirts, one black, the other a bright yellow. A floppy hat with black flowers tumbled from her head, revealing dark brown, shoulder-length hair.

Catching her had been an easy task. She couldn't outrun his wolf. That he'd caught her holding a candle to a frame while, feet away, flames ate a curtain and teased the carpet had been a bonus.

"She set the fire. Don't let her get away!" Markus instructed, turning and heading back to the exit.

"Hey, wait!" The enforceman handed the woman off to another guardian. "You can't just say that and leave. We need the accusations, or we can't hold her."

"I'm accusing her of arson, of this establishment and ten others. She's been using aliases, which I'm sure when compared together, will show the same person wrote the names the day all the fires were started. We even believe we know why."

The woman squeaked.

Markus pointed at her. "If anything happens to my wife—"

Hurry, we must hurry! Lunah barked, jumping in place.

Markus had also felt Bella's panic. Her fear. Her sorrow.

"Lunah, *straes'ya*," he commanded, without knowing where Bella had gone inside the building. Their mated bond would give him a general sensation, but not like his wolf could manage. Lunah would seek her out and show him without error.

She yipped and dashed to the door. Markus yanked it open. Smoke and heat billowed past. He shielded his face and pressed ahead, following Lunah. She ran to an area marked for stage nine, down a corridor to the right, only to backtrack and rush to the adjacent hall.

Blocked, the way to her is blocked! She bayed high pitched and frantic.

Do you know if she's trapped in a corridor or the stage area?

I do not know, I do not! Find her, find her, find my Bella, find her!

Markus fisted his hands and closed his eyes. He couldn't center his thoughts on a deep breath, the smoke was too thick, the air too polluted. Instead, he focused on his beautiful mate. He searched deep, sought out their connection, and followed the delicate thread, wishing he could see through walls. He'd check the stage first, and if that failed, he'd figure a way to get to the corridor.

He grabbed a brass candlestick from a hall table, throwing the doused candle to the floor. The owner's hand-held water shot didn't do much once the curtains and the walls caught fire. Fire services were on the way, but Markus couldn't wait for them. He yanked the curtain down from the first viewing room he came to and kicked the chairs into the corridor. At the glass, he slammed the metal mass into the pane. A star bloomed across the surface. He banged at the glass again. The panel shattered, raining glass between the two rooms.

"Bella!" he shouted. He kicked shards of glass free and stepped into the stage area. "Bella, are you in here?"

"O-over… h-here…" a weak voice croaked.

Using the bond like barometer, he pivoted to the right, where he felt Bella the strongest. He rushed to the corner, where two figures were huddled, slumped against the wall. Kneeling, he touched her face and slid his hand to her throat. The too-fast, thready pulse feathered against his fingertips. Markus gathered her into his arms. She moaned and shifted, agitated.

"Shh," he whispered, his mouth pressed to her temple. "I have you."

"W-wil-willow."

"You first."

She tried to fight free again.

Markus growled. "Stubborn woman."

He tossed her over his shoulder, gathered Willow, and threw her over his other. Grasping the legs of both women, he struggled through the open window. Flames licked at the corridor, and he dashed for the exit, Lunah on his heels. Black smoke roiled, blocking his vision. Lunah took the lead. The golden thread of their bond became his guide.

Cool, fresh air rushed around him as he stumbled outside, gasping in deep gulps. Falling to his knees, both women rolled from his arms. Markus reached weakly for Bella. She coughed and retched, rolling onto her side.

"Willow!" a man shouted. Skidding across

the brick, C.G. fell to his knees. He grabbed at the curtain wrapped around Willow. "Willow, open your eyes, come on."

Markus crawled away from the door, taking Bella with him. Boots pounded on the brick, joining rushed and urgent voices. Fire services had finally arrived. He collapsed against the exterior brick wall, hauling his mate onto his lap. Bella continued to wheeze and cough, but she breathed, and she was conscious. The same could not be said for Willow. Markus rolled his head to the side and watched C.G. attempt to revive his wife.

"Is she... breathing?" Markus panted, his throat dry and aching.

"I don't, I can't..." C.G.'s hands fluttered above his spouse's still form. "I'm not, I don't..."

Lunah, does the woman breathe? Does she live?

His wolf padded to the performer and shoved her nose into the woman's neck. *Lives, she lives. Weak, heart is weak.*

"She needs... a... medical scientist," Markus dropped his head back and hugged Bella to his chest, coughing. "They both... do."

"She-she's alive?" C.G. asked, scooting away from the activity at the door and pulling Willow. The poor woman's arms flopped, and the curtain threatened to be dragged free of her torso.

"Dak."

"Is anyone else in the building?" a deep voice asked.

Markus tilted his head back and stared at a man clothed in thick, bright green canvas. A matching metal helmet sat atop the fire serviceman's head. The burn in Markus's lungs began to ease. "Not that I'm aware."

The serviceman stuck his fingers in his mouth and whistled, then waved. "Over here! We have two!"

A woman carrying a black bag ran to them. She slid to a stop and knelt. "I'm Kerri, a M.S. What can you tell me? Just smoke inhalation?"

"That I know," Markus said, his arms tightening around his mate.

Kerri's gaze missed nothing. "May I touch her?"

"*Dak.*"

The medical scientist gave him a quizzical stare. Markus went to open his mouth, always forgetting to speak *yes* or *no* in Sziverian.

"Yes," Bella croaked.

Kerri nodded and eased her hand to Bella. Gently, she turned his wife's face toward the nearest light source. "There's a small cut here, it doesn't look too serious." Releasing Bella's chin, she dug around inside her pack and pulled out a jar with a pump and an odd mask attached. Holding the top of the jar, she pumped the top and held out the mask. "You pump like this and hold this part to her face. It'll force clean oxygen into her."

Markus accepted the oxygen jar and arranged Bella in his arms. Kerri turned her focus to Willow. Careful to keep Bella upright,

Markus positioned the mask over her nose and mouth and slowly pumped. She took a deep breath and grabbed for the mask.

"Hold it yourself, but don't remove it, okay, *krahet'sna?*" he said, kissing her smoke-saturated curls.

Though she trembled, she kept the mask on her face, taking deep, slow breaths.

"That's it," he encouraged, kissing her again. Lunah lay between his parted legs and rested her muzzle on Bella's stomach. "You scared us."

"The way out," she said, muffled through the mask and paused by deep breathing, "was blocked. We tried everything. To get out."

Markus kept a steady flow of air to her. With each assisted breath, she grew stronger. Steadier. Pushing the mask away, she coughed and tried to sit up. Lunah scrambled backward, and Markus set down the glass jar to help Bella.

"Willow?" she asked.

Markus motioned to the right, where Kerri still worked on the young performer. C.G. held his wife to his chest, her body between his legs. Kerri was nodding, and Willow's eyes appeared to be trying to flutter open.

"Did you get her?" Bella asked, reaching for the oxygen. "Did you get the arsonist?"

Markus handed her the jar and helped her get another clean breath. "*Dak*, we did. She was still setting the fires."

"I hope she confesses. And we don't have to

bring. Forth accusations," Bella said, collapsing against his chest.

"If we do, most of the business owners, including Mr. Weldon, will provide anything enforcement services requires."

She pushed the jar away, sighed, and then coughed. "I'm just glad it's finally over."

EPILOGUE

A week and a half later...

"Did you find my—"

Bella lifted Markus's favorite blue shirt and waved it at him before dropping it into the chest. He was almost finished packing. Her stomach knotted helping him. She didn't want him to leave. They'd had four amazing months together. How was she going to fall asleep without him? The ship carrying him back to his home nation was departing around five this evening. They had under an hour to get out the door and to the MagnaRail station, where a train would take them the rest of the journey to Port Scarbrough.

Bella spun in a circle, lifting a finger. "Did you—"

He held up Lunah's well-loved little purple stuffed animal. "Anything else?"

She opened her mouth to answer when a

heavy knock on the door echoed from the front. Both of them froze.

"Should we answer it?" she asked, whispering and feeling silly for doing so. They were in the bedroom. No one would hear their conversation across the apartment. "We handled all the questions for Mr. Weldon and enforcement services."

"Then it might not be Mr. Weldon or enforcement services," Markus said, squeezing her shoulder as he walked past and out of their bedroom.

Bella sputtered and followed him. She didn't want anyone interrupting the last few precious minutes she had with her husband. Selfish of her? Yes. Lunah stood at the door, quiet and alert. Markus made a hand motion, and the wolf repositioned herself out of the line of sight.

"Hi," a female voice said, "so sorry to bother you, but I heard you were leaving soon?"

Bella moved to stand beside Markus. Willow noticed her and gave a little wave, her cheeks pinkening. "Oh, hello, um, Bella, right?"

"Right. Can we help you?" Bella asked, sliding her fingers between Markus's.

A strand of black hair fell across her forehead, and Willow quickly swept it to the side. "I just, I wanted to say thank you."

Markus stepped back and pulled Bella with him. "Please, come inside."

"Where is C.G.?" Bella asked.

Willow stuffed her hands into her light pink princess jacket. "Cedar had to work today, but I told him I'd be coming. I'm a neighbor now."

"You were able to secure an apartment, congratulations," Bella said.

A deeper flush brightened her cheeks, and she smiled. "I was. On the third floor. I didn't think I'd be able to. I thought I'd only be able to save enough for a second-floor home, but the owner, well, I guess he wants families in the building, so he offered me a discount."

Markus closed the door and returned Willow's smile. "That's great."

"Thank you. I'm very excited."

"C.G. will be renewing his contract with you, then?" Bella asked, a spark of hope for her friend making her want to cross her fingers.

"Um...." Willow laughed weakly and pushed a lock of hair off her forehead again. "Well, I hope so, but I've told him it's unnecessary. I recently learned I'm pregnant, and I couldn't possibly spend eighteen years with someone who would be miserable. Our contract is up in two months."

Bella's eyes widened. "You'd raise the baby alone?"

A faint smile graced Willow's full lips. "Not alone, no. Cedar would be as involved as he'd wish if he chooses not to contract with me again. He could even live in the apartment with me when he isn't contracted to someone else. I love him, and I probably always will, but that's my problem. Again, I just came to thank you. Neither of us knew, but you saved two of us that night."

"Why would you do that?" Markus asked, crossing his arms over his chest.

Willow angled her head to the right. "Do what?"

"Let him be so involved when he isn't willing to make you a true family."

The smile in Willow's eyes turned sad. "I'm a Faneline. A genuine orphan. I know nothing of my family. Not anyone. The moment I became pregnant, I became a family. A part of something amazing, whether Cedar renews his contract with me or not. And he'll be a father, contract or not, and our child will know him."

"He is lucky to have you," Markus said. "I hope he realizes that."

"I hope so, too." Willow rested her hand on her stomach under the knotted tie of her jacket.

Bella resisted the urge to brush her fingers along her lower abdomen. "Congratulations on the baby and the apartment."

Willow's smile widened. "Thank you, again, for making it all possible. If you hadn't come for me...."

Bella grasped her hand and squeezed. "But I did, and we're both fine. More than fine. I hope C.G. is smart enough to realize what he's found with you."

"Well, I think he'd be a fool to leave behind a beautiful apartment in the best part of town," Willow stated, laughing, "but I'll have it without him if that's the case."

"I think he'd be a fool to leave behind a beautiful woman, no matter where in town she lives," Bella whispered, giving Willow's hand one more squeeze before releasing.

"Maybe we can walk together, in the winter months, downstairs," Willow said.

"I'd really like that." And Bella meant the words. She would enjoy some friend time during the depths of winter. Another benefit of living in an apartment versus a home. More ways to socialize.

Bella saw Willow out while Markus went to finish preparing his chest for the voyage. In the corridor, Willow paused and turned. "Did you learn why? The reason that woman started the fire? It was a woman, wasn't that what the paper said? They haven't reported on her motive."

"That's because her accusation hearing hasn't happened yet," Bella answered, holding the edge of the door. "Her lover died of an HRS incident. Three weeks after the worst of the snow had melted, he found a new lover or two and contracted the virus. She said if he'd never gone to the curtain show houses and had an easy way to find a private room, she wouldn't have lost him."

"That's just silly. He'd have taken a lover anywhere he wanted. Most people who come to curtain show houses are looking for a way to remain responsible citizens while still having a little thrill."

"I know. I think she just needed a reason to blame his infidelity and his loss."

"Sad."

Bella agreed and waved her goodbyes. Inside, Markus dragged the chest out by the handle, the little wheels on the corners squeaking in protest, his backpack slung over a shoulder. Bella wanted to sit on the floor and cry. She willed away her dramatic longing. Fits of despair weren't something she usually felt, let alone indulged.

"It's the bond," he whispered, his fingers brushing her neck. "Being apart will be difficult."

"How do we handle it?" she asked, concerned for them and what the next weeks would do to their relationship.

He kissed her throat beneath her ear and whispered, "One day at a time."

FIVE HOURS LATER...
Port Scarbrough

BELLA BRUSHED curls from her face. The salty ocean breeze flew them right back across her eyes and into her mouth. Seagulls squawked and bickered above, fighting over food and spaces to land. The bright sun gleamed off the white sails of the ship bound for Ruthenia. A porter accepted tickets from passengers, welcoming them onboard and giving instructions to their quarters.

Markus turned to her, and Bella lifted her face, prepared for a kiss goodbye. Grabbing her hands, he fell to his knees, and she gasped in surprise.

"What are you doing?" she asked.

"Tell me now," he said, his gaze searching hers, his thumbs caressing the backs of her hand.

Confused, she blinked. "Tell you what?"

"About our baby. Tell me now before I leave."

"Markus..."

"I will go crazy wondering. I know, in my heart, the truth, but I need to hear the words."

"But, what if I'm not?" Her heart clenched, and she sank to the wooden dock with him. "What if something happens?"

"Then we'll handle that together when I radio or return home. But I want to hear you say it. I want to touch you when you speak the words."

"But I don't know if I am," she insisted.

"Trust me," he whispered, bringing her hand to his chest and pressing it over his pounding heart, "you are. Tell me."

In five days, she'd know for certain, for she'd miss her monthly. In five days, he'd already be in Ruthenia, doing whatever they required of him. More than likely, as he predicted, nothing would happen on the day her bleeding should start. For the first time in a decade, she'd not need to wear the ridiculous but necessary thick underwear more reminiscent of a diaper than a pair of panties. Because a baby would be growing within her.

Taking a deep breath, she flexed her fingers into the warmth of his chest, wishing she were touching his skin. His fingers tunneled under her hair at the base of her neck. He rested his forehead on hers. Tears stung her eyes. "Markus... I'm pregnant."